i

THE DAUNTING

Kurt James

DEDICATION:
I would like to dedicate this book to my brother Dane. From the time I was little, he in his way always protected me from a childhood that had more unpleasant memories than pleasant ones. He was and still is my hero.

ACKNOWLEDGMENTS:
I want to thank my lifelong friend and fellow Sheridan Ram Kurt "Wally" Wollenweber who without his continuing support I could not fulfill my dream of being a storyteller.
I would also like to thank my co-worker and friend Rick Paulsen for his efforts in helping me fine tune my work of fiction.

Disclaimer:
This is a work of fiction. Names, characters, businesses,
places, events and incidents are either the products of
the author's imagination or used in a fictitious manner.
Any resemblance to actual persons, living or dead, or
actual events is purely coincidental.

KURT JAMES

TABLE OF CONTENTS

THE DAUNTING

CHAPTER 1

I was deep in thought and sitting on the side of Highway 40 just a mile or so northwest of Kremmling, Colorado letting my 1975 four wheel drive K5 Chevy Blazer with the stick shift in neutral purr almost soundlessly with its 350 cubic inches of raw power.

My Friday shift had been uneventful so far, and my work day was fast coming to an end on this sunny yet cold September day. Autumn and its cooler temperatures were foretelling of the high mountain bitter cold and snow that was not far off and was the norm for Grand County, Colorado. I sort of chuckled once again recalling what the locals called the seasons here at 8,000 feet in Grand County - "summer, winter, and mud season." That saying was coined way before I was ever born, but there never was a truer phrase of living life in the Rocky Mountains.

I smiled as I reached down to turn up the radio as one of Waylon Jennings' older songs came on; it reminded me of my girlfriend. Enjoying the thoughts and the song, I sang along to "Good Hearted Woman." I love Waylon and of course Willie Nelson and their new brand of outlaw country music. I was even getting Nickey Lynn to the point that she could almost stand it. *"Through teardrops and laughter, they'll pass through this world hand-in-hand..."*

I rolled down my window because the hot air blowing from the heat defroster was stale and stifling. Getting the much needed fresh air, I looked northeast up Muddy Creek thinking Nickey and I both had the weekend off and that I might just be able to talk her into some fishing on Sunday. Saturday we were busy since the high school football team in Granby was playing at home, and we liked to show our Middle Park Panther pride by going. So Sunday would be the free day for fishing at one of our lakes either Lake Granby, Shadow Mountain Lake, or maybe make the fifteen mile drive to Grand Lake. She would vote for Grand Lake since they had those tourist shops she liked to browse through. It didn't matter much to me if we fished or not, just so long as I got to spend my day with Nickey.

Just thinking of Nickey sets my blood on fire. I had never met a woman like her before. She was thirty and of Mexican descent, intelligent, and had a great sense of humor, and of course she has those eyes! Her eyes were brown with a hint of blue which of course was just icing on the cake as they complemented her natural beauty. Her hair was shoulder length and midnight black on her 5'8" slender frame, and I loved to hold her hair in my hand right before we would go to sleep. Of course, when awake, it was difficult not to stare as she walked away because her butt was a total class act all by itself. She was by far the most beautiful woman I had ever met and it made me proud that she saw fit to spend her time with me. Mi Vida was her nickname that her mom had given her back home in Phoenix, Arizona which meant "my life" in Spanish. Thinking of Nickey as Mi Vida seemed rather fitting for me as well as Nickey had become "my life." She had moved here to Grand County about two years ago, and we met at work. Her first and middle names are Nickey and Lynn, and I called her both Nickey and Nickey Lynn.

While enjoying the fresh air, I saw in the side mirror of the Blazer a car approaching fast behind me - way too fast - heading eastbound on Highway 40. It was not unusual as folks spent more time than they like going over the winding road of Rabbit Ears Pass summit, so they tried to make up lost time on the flat highway just northwest of Kremmling. I reached out my left arm and slowly waved it up and down so they would get the hint and slow down. It would not be good for them to barrel roll through the town of

Kremmling and endanger any of the kids that ride their stingrays with sissy bars on the highway as they often do.

The reckless oncoming car behind me was not slowing down, and I put my right hand on the stick shift with my foot hanging over the clutch just in case they did not get the hint.

They blew right on past me doing at least ninety. As they flew by, I got a good glimpse of the passenger as he had his pointy finger and thumb pressed together in the classic stoner ritual of toking on a joint.

I shook my head and blinked my eyes several times thinking that they must be really stoned not to see the lights on top and the painted decal on the side of my Blazer indicating they just passed a standing still Grand County Sheriff's officer.

Turning off Waylon and the radio and turning on my lights and siren, I quickly floored the clutch and shifted into 2nd, spinning the tires on the gravel as I pulled out onto Highway 40 to pursue. I speed shifted through 3rd and then into 4th gear.

Grabbing the radio microphone, I depressed the call button with my right thumb and said, "Dispatch, this is Dane Lee and be advised I am in pursuit of a brand new blue and white 1976 Cobra II Mustang heading at a high rate of speed eastward through Kremmling heading in your direction."

Yvonne Patterson the dispatcher for the county quickly countered with, "All cars be advised that Undersheriff Lee is in pursuit of a 1976 blue and white Mustang and is heading east on Highway 40."

By the time I reached the west side of Kremmling, the Mustang had already blown by 6th street and was not slowing down. Quickly scanning the side streets for kids on bikes and stray dogs and seeing none, I slowly increased my speed as the Mustang exited on the east side of the town. Just as I exited the east side as well, the radio crackled and a voice I knew all too well said, "Dane did you say a 1976 Cobra II?"

Laughing out loud, I knew that would get Chavez' attention. Keying the microphone once more, "Yes Officer Chavez, it was a 1976 Mustang Cobra II the full package with the black grille, hood scoop, front and rear spoilers, quarter window louvers, and accent stripes. You would love it. Also, it had Colorado plates but was going so fast I did not get a copy on them as it blew by me."

Officer Chavez keyed the microphone again and my radio crackled, "Dane, I have my Blazer started and leaving the office now heading westbound on Highway 40. I am so excited about seeing the new Mustang I spilled my coffee in my lap."

Keying my microphone once again, "Copy that Chavez. Be advised at least two suspects possibly more in the Mustang. They probably will be impaired because they were smoking a joint when they passed me."

Yvonne piped in, "Must be Denver kids; Grand County kids can't afford fancy cars like that and are at least smart enough to park and smoke."

If Officer Chavez was heading in my direction from the office, which was located at the county seat in Hot Sulphur Springs which was only 17 miles away, this was going to be a short pursuit. Keying my mic, "I have lost sight of the Mustang. Officer Chavez what is your 20?"

Nothing but static on the sheriff's band radio. Keying the microphone once again, "Repeat, Officer Chavez, I have lost sight of suspects. What is your 20?"

There was still static and empty airwaves as I was fast approaching the little town of Parshall in between Kremmling and Hot Sulphur Springs. It was less than a minute later I got my answer about the whereabouts of Officer Chavez. The 1976 Mustang was off to the right side of the road, and two young boys about sixteen or seventeen with long brown scraggly hair, wearing Rolling Stones tee-shirts were handcuffed and leaning against the back of officer Chavez' Grand County Sheriff's Chevy Blazer.

Pulling up alongside of the other Blazer, I opened the door and stepped out and immediately got a substantial whiff of the burnt weed that the two young men had been enjoying. The Mustang was being aired out with the driver's door half opened. I said, looking at Chavez, "Not even sure why I work here since I never get to do any of the fun stuff anymore."

Officer Chavez walked over and handed me a baggie full of about three ounces of pot. "Here is your evidence Dane and just remember you are the boss and the thinker, so the peons like myself in the department have to do all the heavy lifting. I got one question though!"

Grinning from ear to ear as I looked at Officer Chavez, "Can't wait to hear what it is?"

Officer Chavez stepped up even closer and then looked back toward the handcuffed boys to make sure no one was looking and stood up on her tiptoes and kissed me before saying, "That's a sweet car and since I caught it, can I keep it?"

Shaking my head and with a small chuckle, "Not on your life, Nickey Lynn."

CHAPTER 2

Looking into those eyes I loved so much, I had to force myself not to get lost in them so after the small kiss we shared, I stepped back from Nickey and reacquired my undersheriff personality since we both were still at work.

Pointing at the two stoned Rolling Stones and weed enthusiasts, I spoke loudly enough so they could hear, "Officer Chavez, take those two punks back to the cooler and lock them up, and I will call for a tow truck to impound the Mustang."

Nickey, with her eyes still glowing from our kiss, faded back into her role as a Grand County Sheriff's officer as well and spoke just as loudly for the young boys to hear, "Consider it done Undersheriff Lee."

Lowering my voice so only Nickey could hear, "Once they are behind bars and sobering up, try and get a hold of their parents and have their folks come and get them. Have the folks or someone pay the impounding fee on the Mustang and then let the boys go with a lot of finger pointing and a stern warning about the evils of hot rodding it through our county high on weed."

Nickey rolled her eyes in the cute way that she does and she also lowered her voice, "That's what I love about my cowboy Dane is that under that gruff exterior beats a heart of gold."

Reaching through the Blazer window, I grabbed my radio microphone and turned back to Nickey Lynn and replied with a smile, "Hey, I am just not a country music fan Mi Vida; I also happen to like the Stones as well - so no harm done! Sober them up, feed them, slap their wrist and send them home."

As Nickey was turning away, she stopped and turned back to face me with that smile of hers. "Dane, what about the weed?"

With smiling eyes, I said, "Incinerate it." Nickey's eyes even got larger so I thought I needed to be clearer. "Incinerate the pot in the station incinerator out back of the station and...do not smoke it."

Nickey Lynn's smile turned into the pouty frown she used when she did not get her way, but with a half chuckle she replied, "Copy that Undersheriff Lee!"

Depressing the key on the microphone, "Dispatch, be advised that Officer Chavez is in route with two suspects in custody. Have the two jailers meet her in the Sally Port for the handoff. Also, get a hold of One Eye Zach and his tow truck out of Granby and tell him I have a 1976 blue and white Mustang with a Colorado license plate that reads SRD 1978. I will wait until he shows up."

Yvonne acknowledged me, "Copy that undersheriff. Calling One Eye now."

Once One Eye Zach had towed the Mustang to the impound yard, I headed the almost six miles back to the sheriff's office in Hot Sulphur Springs. As I turned up the radio, an Eddie Rabbitt song "Rocky Mountain Music" started playing. *"Rocky mountain music fills my memory..."*

Hearing this song for the first time, I was reminded of my home here in Grand County. Of course growing up here in the mountains, you learn the history of the place you call home. Grand County was 1,868 square miles in size and was created February 2, 1874 and was named after Grand Lake and the Grand River, the original name of the upper Colorado River. Some of the towns in the county were Grand Lake, Hot Sulphur Springs, Parshall, Kremmling, Winter Park, Fraser, Tabernash, and of course Granby where I lived with Nickey. Grand County and its towns also resided in what was called Middle Park. The two major highways that connected Grand County and Middle Park to the rest of the world were Highway 40 and Highway 34.

Middle Park is a high mountain basin with the bottom being just as flat as western Colorado, but surrounded on all sides, creating the basin and bowl by the snow-capped mountains. To travel out of Grand County or Middle Park, you had to traverse one of the many high mountain passes depending in what direction you were going.

Middle Park was close to 1,000 square miles in size and was one of three types of high mountain basins in Colorado with the one in the north part of the state called North Park and of course the one south of Middle Park was simply called South Park. To the north of Granby and Grand Lake were some of the most remote wilderness areas in the world within the boundaries of Rocky Mountain National Park.

Rocky Mountain National Park consisted of about a half million acres of federal and forest service land that was situated between the towns of Estes Park to the east and Grand Lake to the west. The eastern and western slopes of the Continental Divide run directly through the center of the park with the headwaters of the Colorado River located in the park's northwestern region. The park has everything an outdoor enthusiast would want - mountains, alpine lakes, and a wide variety of wildlife within various climates and environments, from wooded forests to mountain tundra. The highest paved road in the world goes from Grand Lake to Estes Park and is named Trail Ridge Road. Just this year some organization named UNESCO started calling Rocky Mountain National Park a "World Biosphere."

I was not sure what a "World Biosphere" actually was, but it sure did sound impressive. All I know is "The Park" is heaven to me.

I had read everything that the naturalist John Muir ever wrote, and the one quote of his that always spoke to me was, "The Mountains are calling, and I must go." Rocky Mountain National Park not only spoke to me, but it was also in my blood. I have Rocky Mountain Ute Indian blood running through my veins. The Grand River Utes called all of Grand County their home before the white man ever showed his pale face here. My great, great, great grandfather was none other than the famed mountain man Matt Lee, whom the Indians called "Ghost." Although Matt Lee was white, he had married my grandmother who was a princess of the Grand River Ute tribe and her name after marrying my grandfather was "Walk With Ghost." Only few people know this about me and I have never told Nickey Lynn; my grandfather visits me in my dreams sometimes and points the way and gives me direction. It seems that the famous Lee "Ghost" only makes visits to the male side of the Lee clan. It would seem that the Lee's were not just born here, but we were also part of the landscape and mystique of the Rocky Mountains.

It was not long until I pulled in to the sheriff's office parking lot. I walked into the office and just like every other time I walked in or out of the squad room, I looked at the missing person photos and flyers tacked on the bulletin board in the main hallway, but examined closely one particular flyer. For over four years now, the photo and description of Micah has hung on this wall with never a good lead in all those years. I read the description even though I knew it by heart:

MICAH TRASK
DOB - 3/12/1945
SEX - MALE
RACE – CAUCASIAN
EYES - BROWN
HAIR - BLACK
HEIGHT - 6' 2"
WEIGHT - 205
MISSING FROM - GRANBY / GRAND COUNTY, COLORADO
MISSING SINCE - 9/16/1972 SATURDAY
IDENTYFING CHARACTERISTICS - MISSING THUMB ON RIGHT HAND
$5000 REWARD
IF ANY INFORMATION PLEASE CONTACT THE GRAND COUNTY SHERIFF'S DEPARTMENT

The $5000 reward was money that I had personally set aside in a bank account and as of this date, no one has ever come forward with any information. Micah's whereabouts were still a mystery. As per my routine each and every time I passed Micah's missing person flyer, I took my forefinger and the finger next to it and pressed Micah's photo for a couple of seconds. It was silly really, but somehow the ritual of touching his photograph made me still care about my best friend that had lost his way.

The squad room was a completely open office with no walls to separate the six office desks and once I settled into mine, I started checking my messages.

Just as I had cleared my desk of all the tasks I needed to complete for the day, Gene Sanford, one of the officers in my command, stopped by my desk and handed me a book. "I picked up that book about your grandfather at Waldenbooks a couple of days ago when I was in Denver."

Curious, I took the book named "Rocky Mountain Ghost" that was written by a fellow named Kurt James and looked at the cover which was a night time photo of a mountain mesa with some snow with a blue moon looking down on the very serene scene. Turning the book over, I read the summary.

"ROCKY MOUNTAIN GHOST"

Matt Lee - a young trapper and mountain man - and his five closest friends, after hearing a tale of lost Spanish gold and the legend La Caverna Del Oro told by an old mysterious mountain man, decided to search for the cave of riches located above timberline on Marble Mountain, Colorado. The five close friends were jovial with their good luck after locating the lost cavern of gold. It would not be long before they realized that the haunted La Caverna Del Oro was protected by a band of Ute Indian warriors whose sole purpose was to prevent anybody from taking the gold and releasing what lived in the depths of the ancient cave. Matt Lee who was the sole survivor of a bloody battle had now stepped over the edge into insanity as the rage and chaos of what lived within the cave became one within him. For the next two years, Matt Lee in his madness would become the Ute Indians' greatest enemy; they started calling him "Ghost." One by one the Ute tribes would send their mightiest warriors against the Ghost. Matt Lee was forever doomed to this fate as the Ute enemy Ghost until a fateful day on a remote pond in the Middle Park Basin of Colorado changed the course of his life once again. Matt Lee stepped back over into the land of the rational the day he rescued a young Ute Indian princess from a mountain lion attack. For the next thirty years, Matt Lee's forever love for his wife Walk With Ghost would keep the madness deep within his soul. Matt Lee and the love of his life just wanted to build their home and find sanctuary far from his haunted and bloody past in a hidden valley on Boreas Pass above the town of Como, Colorado - Redemption Valley. That would all change when Walk With Ghost was shot by a member of the Colorado 3rd U.S. Cavalry on the streets of Grand Lake, Colorado. Little did the U.S. Cavalry know that they had once again unleashed the legend known as "Ghost!" Follow this Kurt James western adventure of redemption and revenge of a man the Indians called "Ghost" as he battles Indians, racial hatred, mountain lions, avalanches, bounty hunters, and federal marshals in such towns and places as Grand Lake, Berthoud Pass, Guanella Pass, and Kenosha Pass of the Rocky Mountain frontier."

Handing the book back to Gene I said, "Matt Lee was my great, great, great, grandfather. I believe he and my grandmother died in the 1880's or 1890's. Grandfather buried my grandmother in the hidden valley called Redemption Valley on Boreas Pass. Soon after grandfather died in a successful rescue attempt of the granddaughter of the famous Marshal Eric Robert, but that is another story altogether."

Gene took the book back as if he was handling a piece of fine china or something and said, "Will do Dane - can't wait to start it this weekend."

What I didn't say to Gene was once I touched the book, I felt an electric shock of sorts and a quick vision flashed through my mind of a cave somewhere in the Rocky Mountains and it was full of bodies. The vision unnerved me some; I knew it was my grandfather Matt Lee reaching out beyond the years and the grave showing me something once again. What he was trying to tell me currently, I did not have a clue.

Still with my thoughts about Micah and my great grandfather, I left the office and made the eleven mile drive home to Granby. Nickey had left earlier and probably already had supper ready. Thank God it was Friday. It had been a long, but uneventful week and I was looking forward to some sack time.

CHAPTER 3

Waking up at 5 a.m. as usual, no matter if it was my day off or not, I was feeling a little drowsy; Nickey had woke me up during the night for some after-hours adult time and thinking about it brought a smile to my face once again. Nickey has been never hard to get, just hard to forget. I thank the stars each and every day I wake up next to this woman. Getting out of bed slowly trying not to disturb the woman I loved and once successful and standing next to the bed, I watched Mi Vida sleep for a spell. It was one of my guilty pleasures I never told her about. True love, it would seem, was just being happy together even if one was asleep.

Stepping into the bathroom and stopping in front of the mirror, I wondered what a woman like Nickey Lynn saw in a man like me. Even though women had always been attracted to me, I was thirty-one years old and never really thought of myself as handsome. I was 6'2'' and weighed 200 pounds and heavily muscled with short dark hair and brown eyes. On a scale of one to ten, I thought I was maybe a six. Nickey thought differently and that was all that really mattered. Nickey always kidded me I had girl eyes because my eyelashes were long. If anyone had said that other than Nickey, I would have been insulted, but when my Mi Vida says it, I feel good.

I worked out four days a week at the high school gym to keep in shape and spent any of my free time up in "The Park" mountain climbing and pushing my body and mind to the limit in my self-styled survival training. My dad was a mountain man through and through just like his father and grandfathers all the way back to Matt Lee. It is in the Lee blood to be one with nature and to understand the wilderness of the Rocky Mountains. The men of Lee had known for generations you never conquer the mountains or the wild; you learn to rejoice in the solitude and all that is nature. With the Lee men, the Rocky Mountains are a part of us and it is who we are; my dad and my grandfathers before believed living a life in the wilderness was the equal of churchgoing.

I looked down at my right leg at the foot long scar from a blown out knee - an injury suffered in my last high school football game of my career. Soon after, I tried to join the military along with Micah, but it was not meant to be. The recent injury kept me out of Vietnam when the government classified me 4-F for military service in 1968. Micah my best friend served two tours and when he came back, he had lost three fingers and his thumb on his left hand. That was minor compared to what he lost from his inner soul over there in the jungle. His experience fighting there in the jungle changed him. He never talked about his time in Vietnam or what he saw. Being his best friend, I never pressed him on it, but when we would spend time in our mountains and "The Park," we were as we used to be back in our youth. Micah used the wilderness and our friendship to heal the mental wounds he brought back from those faraway jungles in Vietnam. Micah went missing four years ago, and I always wondered if it had to do with what happened to him in Vietnam. I miss my friend - I miss our brotherhood.

As I looked at the clock, it always seemed time flew on Nickey's and my days off and I jumped into the shower to get ready for the day ahead. Today was the big home game against the number one ranked AA team in the state the Sheridan Rams, who were undefeated after two games, just like our own Middle Park Panthers. The Panthers were in the Metro League, which was sort of confusing since most of the teams were from the Denver area; nevertheless, that is the league they played in. Middle Park had beaten Mapleton High and Holy Family by narrow margins. Sheridan, on the other hand, had blown out Denver Lutheran and

Clear Creek High. The Sheridan Rams were a juggernaut and the hometown Panthers were the underdogs. There were purple and white panther prints, the school emblem, everywhere in town for weeks with pride in the team's winning ways. Almost everyone in town would be attending the game.

I woke Nickey up at nine with a breakfast of scrambled eggs and bacon and a piece of lightly burnt toast just as she liked it. This simple breakfast was the only type of cooking that Nickey trusted me to make. As we dressed, I looked outside to gauge the weather, and it was sunny and cool just like most September days in Grand County. Nickey and I both wore our Wrangler jeans, pearl button Wrangler flannel shirts, and matching belts, except mine had been stamped Dane and hers had been stamped Nickey on the back of the belt. After stomping into our everyday Tony Lama cowboy boots, I looked at the woman that shared my life and reveled in the transformation that she had gone through since she moved from the big city of Phoenix to Granby. She may have been raised in the city, but she was a Rocky Mountain cowgirl through and through.

Since my job called for me to be on duty 24/7, I belted on my 357 3-screw Ruger Blackhawk as we grabbed our goose down Tempco coats as we headed out the door. Nickey never carried her Ruger when she was off duty. As we jumped into my county K5 Blazer, we had one chore to do first before heading to the ball field.

Turning on the radio my favorite Linda Ronstadt song "Love is a Rose" was playing and Nickey and I naturally joined in and sang along with Linda as if we were the only ones in the world that knew the lyrics. *"I want to see what's never been seen..."*

I turned west on Agate which was Highway 40 until I ran into the crossroad of Highway 34 which headed north towards Grand Lake and eventually Rocky Mountain National Park. I then turned north for a short hop until we reached the dirt road at Smith Creek that headed back east again until we reached the barn where we boarded our horses.

Cochise who was Nickey's three year old gelding Appaloosa was the first out of the barn and pacing the corral fence in anticipation of some time with Nickey. Cochise's chest and front legs were ebony black and his hindquarters looked as if someone had spilled twenty gallons of white paint which gave him the most beautiful mixture of black and snow I had ever seen on a horse. He was gentle and about fifteen hands high and was the perfect size for Nickey. Cochise barely tolerated me but loved Nickey Lynn like no other.

Thunder my mare finally came out of the barn and made her way to the corral fence as well, and she pawed and snorted a few times when she saw me. She was slightly bigger than Cochise at sixteen hands and all Mustang. She was all tan except for her front forelegs which had white as snow stockings and a white star on her forehead. I had adopted her from the Bureau of Land Management a couple of years ago when she was a year old, and I took a considerable amount of time and more than a few bumps and bruises to break her to a saddle. Once I quit trying to be her master and instead to become equal to her in terms of temperament is when she let me finally ride her. Her wild horse instincts still will let no one get close enough to even try to put a saddle on her except me. She was and always will be a one man horse. Somehow that seemed fitting to me.

Every day Nickey or I made this trip to feed and groom our horses. In our hectic daily lives, we didn't get to ride them as much as we would like, but our love for Cochise and Thunder could not have been any stronger. They were part of our family.

After caring for the horses, we headed east until we came to county road 61 and then south until we got to the high school football field. The small stadium was standing room only with Panther purple and white on the home side, and the visitor side was filled with the blue and silver of the Sheridan Rams.

We lost the coin toss and the Sheridan Rams elected to receive the ball as Nickey and I made our way to the sidelines to the only place left to watch the game. Number 22 of the Rams received the ball and with more speed than any other kid on the field ran the kickoff back for the first score of the game without ever being touched as he ran down the sideline right in front of Nickey and myself. It would seem that the number one rating of Sheridan was not a fluke. By the end of the first quarter it was Sheridan 28 and Middle Park 0. The Rams were formidable with considerable speed in their backfield and plenty of lightning up front in the offensive line. The kid who played QB for Sheridan was named Kurt Wollenweber and he never threw a pass in the whole first half, but between him and the rest of the backfield, they racked up over 300 yards of offense and at halftime the score was 42 to zip and the game was painful to watch.

Nickey and I were standing next to the concession stand drinking a Coke and eating a hot dog when Yvonne the dispatcher for the county walked over and handed me a folded note and then said, "Dane before I left the sheriff's office, Grand Lake Plumbing called in something they thought was a bit different. It would seem that they had been called out for a no heat call on a hot water boiler last Saturday and when their plumber got there, no one was home and someone locked the door. They have tried calling and checking back each day for a week, and the person who had called about no heat seems nowhere to be found. Frank, the owner is worried with the weather turning cold that the building will freeze up so he thought maybe someone from our department could run by and check."

Taking the note and feeling a little confused why Yvonne thought this was important enough to track me down at the ball game, I shrugged my shoulders and said, "Gene is on duty today; why didn't you have him check this out?"

Yvonne's eyes narrowed before she spoke. "Look at the address. I thought you might want to run by and check it out yourself."

Still kind of confused, I opened the note, and the address read - 191 E Agate Ave. Nickey was now looking at the note as well and she read the address out loud. "191 E Agate Avenue. I don't get it. Why is this address important?"

Turning from looking at Yvonne and then looking at Nickey, I said, "That address is a business building on Main Street with an apartment above and the last place I ever saw Micah Trask. It is Micah's old fly-fishing shop and home."

CHAPTER 4

Feeling guilty about running out on the Panthers' butt kicking by the Sheridan Rams, Nickey and I at least had a legit reason for ducking out. Once we had gotten back to the Blazer, it was only a few minutes since Granby was such a small town before we were sitting at 2nd and Agate.

I parked the county Blazer on the west side of the two story building in an empty lot next to the building that Micah four years ago called work and home and facing south toward the Blue Spruce Motel on the south side of Agate.

Looking at the two story gray brick building, I remembered Saturday 9/16/1972 just as if it was yesterday. We sat in the Blazer for a full minute as I stared at the building to the east before Nickey spoke, "Tell me about it, Dane."

Still staring at Micah's old place of business that also served as his home, "Not much to tell Nickey. Last time I saw Micah was right here on a Friday evening on 9/15/1972; we had spent a couple of hours fishing at Lake Granby that evening with not much luck and we came home with no fish. Micah had planned on going to Rocky Mountain National Park the next day on Saturday and do some hiking by himself since it was a work day for me and his day off. He went missing that day, and no one has seen hide nor hair of him since."

Nickey spoke almost to herself as she tried to put sense into Micah's disappearance. "People disappear in Rocky Mountain National Park all the time. Just last week we had that middle-aged couple from Denver that went for a walk and never came back."

Turning to look at Nickey, "I know it happens all the time - most people are unprepared for the wilderness and lose their way in the mountains and the mountains claim them as their own - but Micah was different. He grew up in these mountains and he fought in the jungle as well. Micah was a cowboy, soldier, and a mountain man. He was as tough as they come, and my gut instinct has always been that the mountains didn't get him - something or someone else did. There is zero evidence that says anything sinister happened to my best friend, but in my heart I know something did. I have never in four years been able to figure out what happened. After all these years I know Micah is dead - this I have no doubt. I just don't know how or why. It will always bother me that I do not know the whole story of what happened to Micah. It breaks my heart."

Opening the doors of the Blazer, Nickey and I both stepped out into the chilly September day. The sky above our heads was blue and full of lazy floating clouds. The temperature was forty degrees and the golden leaves on the aspens were still in their death struggle as autumn was in full swing.

As we approached the front, there were two forest green painted doors on the east side of the front entrance and one on the west side. There also were two half whiskey barrel flower planters stationed on each side with the flowers long dead since the weather had turned colder. The building had been set up to be two different businesses but since I could remember, it only housed one. The door on the west was locked and had a sign that said, "Use Other Door." The east door that had a hand-painted message read "Craig Dale Wilderness Photographer." I knocked three times and then I tried the doorknob and it was locked. Standing back, I studied the building as Nickey put both of her hands and her face against the glass of the door trying to peer inside as she spoke to me, "Driven by here more times than I can count but had never been inside. Do you know Craig Dale?"

Looking up at the second floor and the window on the right, which used to serve as Micah's living room, I replied to Nickey,

"Talked to him a couple of times. He is a little older than I am and had served in Vietnam like Micah. He moved here from Belle Fourche, South Dakota to be closer to The Park so he could do his wildlife and nature photography. I think he was also branching out and was writing a book of some sort. He like Micah and myself enjoyed the wilderness and spent considerable time up in Rocky Mountain National Park."

Bending down, I tipped the planter on the east up and found a shiny chrome key there. Nickey started to laugh, "How did you know that key was there?"

As I picked it up, "Micah kept one there because he was always locking himself out. Kind of surprised it is still there myself after all these years. Now to find out if Craig Dale ever changed the lock."

The key inserted smoothly and the well-oiled deadbolt snapped back into the door with a solid thump. Pocketing the key and drawing my 3 screw 357 Ruger, I slowly opened the front door, speaking out loud, "Mr. Dale are you here? Craig, it is Dane Lee of the Grand County Sheriff's office. We are concerned about you and I am entering the building now."

As I stepped into the front room of the business, two things stood out: one it was damn cold in here since the heat was off just as the plumber had said, and two there was this guy that was one hell of a wildlife photographer. The walls of his gallery were full of framed prints of his work and being a man of the wilderness myself, I was impressed with his shots of elk, mountain lions, and bighorn sheep. It would seem he had a talent for capturing the moon and it arc over the Rocky Mountains. There was a small sink next to a table on the first floor, and I walked over and turned on the water and it flowed easily from the tap. At least the building had not frozen up yet.

Nickey was still standing in the gallery admiring Mr. Dale's photography when I said, "Could you use the radio in the truck and have dispatch call Frank from Grand Lake Plumbing and see if he has a service man available. I would hate for this place to freeze and then thaw out and flood and damage all of these photos. Have them tell Frank if he is worried about payment and Mr. Dale doesn't pay that the county will make the bill good somehow."

As Nickey walked out of the building, I started up the back stairs to the apartment I knew so well on the second floor with my Ruger still drawn. The boards creaked with each step and announced with each stair as I was walking up them, but I still said out loud once again, "Mr. Dale, I am now heading up the stairs to the top floor. Are you up there?"

No sound from above as I made my way to the top of the stairs. It was slightly warmer here as what heat there was in the building naturally rose to the highest level. I stepped into what used to be Micah's living room, and the walls here as they were below had many photos of wildlife, mountains, and sunrises and sunsets. Near the window was a desk and on top in the middle of hundreds of pages of typewritten paper was a bright yellow brand new Smith Corona electric typewriter. Seeing that the room was empty, I moved to the bedroom which had a made up double bed. I checked the bathroom and the spare bedroom that had been turned into a dark room for developing photos. Micah's old business and apartment looked nothing like it had before Micah had disappeared. Of course, everything that had been Micah's had long been removed by his family, and they had sold the building to Craig Dale. With nothing of Micah still here in this building, it drove home the fact that my friend was never coming home.

Just as that thought crossed my mind, I heard Nickey's footsteps downstairs, and she said loudly, "Dane, are you upstairs?"

Replying loud enough for her to hear, "All clear Officer Chavez!"

As Nickey reached the top of the stairs, she saw all the photographs on the wall and stopped to look at Mr. Dale's obvious talent of capturing nature at its finest. "This Craig guy is one damn good photographer."

Turning to look at Nickey Lynn and admiring how her Wrangler jeans hugged her bottom and with a smile on my face, "That he is Officer Chavez. The question is not if Mr. Dale knows his way around a camera or not. The question is where the hell is he?"

Still looking at the photos on the wall, Nickey chuckled and said, "Undersheriff Lee, I can feel you staring at my butt."

Shaking my head, knowing I was guilty as charged, "Technically, my love, we are both off today and I can stare at that fine piece of machinery if I want to. Did dispatch get ahold of Grand Lake Plumbing?"

Mi Vida turned in my direction with a huge smile on her face. "Frank the owner is sending over a man to work on getting some heat in here. And since we are both off today Mr. Lee, I do in fact give you permission to stare at my butt."

I laughed out loud this time; there was no doubt that I loved this woman and I would gladly take a bullet to protect her if it was her life or mine. "Duly noted on both counts, Officer Chavez."

Walking over to the desk and touching nothing, "It looks like Mr. Dale has in fact started his book."

Next to the Smith Corona electric typewriter was a stack of about 200 double spaced typewritten pages with a cover sheet stating the name of his book "The Daunting" by Craig Dale.

Looking to the left of "The Daunting" stack of pages was a single page that had seven names and all had dates next to them except the top one.

Samael Amos
Bryan Amen 9/27/1975 SATURDAY
Jerry Toney 10/5/1974 SATURDAY
Randy Weems 9/8/1973 SATURDAY
Shawn Lord 10/13/1973 SATURDAY
Kevin Kyriss 10/21/1972 SATURDAY
Micah Trask 9/16/1972 SATURDAY

I stared at the last name on the list and knowing the date by heart – the day Micah disappeared – I spoke out loud to no one, "What the hell?"

CHAPTER 5

Moving alongside of me, Nickey Lynn read the list of names as well touching nothing. "Besides Micah, do you know any of these names, Dane?"

Shaking my head "no" and with some confusion in my voice and reading the list twice, I kept coming back to the first name at the top. "I have never heard of the name Samael. Do you think it is supposed to be Samuel and just misspelled?"

Nickey began to read the name out loud, "Samael Amos, no Samael is spelled correctly - it is a Jewish name."

Now more confused than ever I looked at Nickey and said, "Jewish? How do you know it is Jewish?"

Looking at me with a huge grin, Nickey replied, "I am half Jewish on my mother's side, and catholic on my father's side. The holidays sort of got confused growing up with my folks."

Still confused as ever I said, "Jewish? I thought you were Mexican? I had no idea there were Mexican Jewish people."

Nickey Lynn smiled and chuckled and then rolled her eyes in that "you don't know shit" look I got from time to time from her. "I am Mexican, but my mom was from New Jersey you dimwit, and New Jersey is full of Jewish people. You really need to get out of the mountains every once in a while. Sometimes I can hear the banjos and fiddles playing in your mind."

That made me laugh out loud. "I like banjos and fiddles, Nickey, and you will learn to love them as well. I have never heard of the name Samael; I wonder what it means."

Nickey stepped in closer and on tiptoes gave me a quick kiss on the cheek. "I already love the banjos and fiddles and the tunes they play in your head, Mr. Undersheriff Lee. And I got the answer to your question as well. Samael is one of the Jewish myths; Samael is the grim reaper and a fallen angel. He is known as a destroyer and a seducer. He is also known by names like the Prince of Darkness and the Chief of the Dragons of Evil."

Thinking about what Nickey had just said and looking at the list for the third time, I could not for the life of me figure out what the Prince of Darkness and the Chief of the Dragons of Evil were doing on the same list as my missing best friend.

As I looked back over the desk once again without touching anything, just in case this ended up being a crime scene, it would seem nothing was out of kilter other than Craig Dale was missing. It reminded me of that Saturday four years ago when I was standing in this exact spot thinking the same thoughts about Micah Trask. The difference between then and now was that I may have a clue and a starting point as I read the list for a fourth time. Of course it could mean absolutely nothing, but my gut instinct told me differently. I could almost feel the ghost of my grandfather standing next to me and pointing at the list. Taking a pen from my front shirt pocket and a sheet of new typing paper from the stack of blank paper in a tray sitting behind the Smith Corona, I copied the names and the dates down in the exact order that Mr. Dale had typed them.

Studying the names once again and looking for a connection of some sort, I heard a voice from downstairs say loudly, "Hello, anyone here? Grand Lake Plumbing."

After introducing ourselves to the service plumber, we let him loose in the building's mechanical room with instructions not to venture out of there or to touch anything else in the building but what was absolutely necessary to fix the heating problem.

Once the plumber was busy with his task of restoring heat to the building, Nickey and I sat in the county Blazer with the heat blasting to stay warm. We had the windows cranked down a tad for fresh air when our neighbor Drew spotted us as he was driving down Agate. He drove behind the building and into the empty lot we were parked on and pulled up next to my window. Drew hand cranked down his window at the same time I cranked mine down all the way so we could talk. Drew started the conversation, "Saw you and Nickey leave at halftime; I suppose you couldn't stomach the slaughter anymore."

Shaking my head, realizing it must have gotten no better for our hometown Panthers once we left, I asked, "We had a welfare check we had to do. What was the final score?"

Drew shook his head in almost disbelief, "56 to nothing. Hell, Sheridan started their junior varsity the second half, and they still scored at will. Those city boys sure know how to play the game of football. After all that hoopla that was happening around town this week in anticipation of this game, it was a silent crowd with barely a peep as they started to leave. Well, got to go, I got a roast in the crock pot that is calling my name."

After Nickey and I said our goodbyes, Drew waved once again and rolled up his window and drove away.

Nickey and I talked about the list more and what it could mean, and we decided we didn't have enough information yet and it would require some more investigative work. The problem was our department really didn't have enough resources for investigative work and did not have a detective on the payroll that was trained in these matters. With all of our other duties, it would be difficult to find the time to track down the meaning of the names and dates on the list. Of course, the mystery could solve itself if Craig Dale showed back up and we could just ask him. I knew in my gut that Mr. Dale, just like Micah, was never coming back. I didn't voice this to Nickey, but I knew it to be true - there would be no help from Craig Dale now or in the future solving the list of mysterious names.

Since Nickey and I were both tired from our late night love making, we both decided to rest our eyes to catch a few winks as we waited for the plumber. Before closing my eyes, I turned the radio on at a low volume and the Eagles song "Lyin' Eyes" was playing…*"There ain't no way to hide…"*

My eyes had been closed just for a few minutes when I was startled by a knock on the driver's side window. Snapping my eyes open and trying to clear the fog from my brain, I realized it was the plumber who had knocked on the window. My hand slipped off the hand crank twice before I could finally get the window down far enough that the plumber could talk. "Got it all fixed, Undersheriff Lee. It was just a loose wire on the circulating pump is all. Already starting to warm up in there. Frank said he would send Mr. Dale a bill in the mail and if it was not paid in thirty days, he would send another bill to the county."

After thanking the plumber from Grand Lake Plumbing, he packed up his tools into his red service truck and left to go home since it was a Saturday. I left a note on the table on the first floor stating that the Grand County Sheriff had been in the building on a welfare check and the plumber had also been in the building repairing the hot water heater and that when Mr. Dale finally got back to please give us a call and let us know that he was okay. I locked the door with Micah's old key and then once again placed the key back under the half whiskey barrel where Micah used to keep it.

The rest of the day was uneventful after Nickey and I had returned home. Nickey kept busy doing chores around the house and getting the fixings together for some real Mexican enchiladas for our supper tonight.

I tried to relax watching television and after getting the rabbit ear antenna just right after moving the tin foil up an inch on the right side, I settled down in my recliner to watch the old Bogart movie Maltese Falcon. Bogart played the detective Sam Spade in the movie and of course had all the best lines. After seeing it in the TV Guide, I had been waiting in anticipation since I loved Humphry Bogart almost as much as I loved John Wayne. I loved the tag line on the Maltese Falcon movie poster *"The stuff that dreams are made of."*

It got to the part in the movie when Sam Spade gave the speech about his partner Archer being killed. *"When a man's partner is killed, he's supposed to do something about it. It doesn't make any difference what you thought of him. He was your partner and you're supposed to do something about it. And it happens, we're in the detective business. Well, when one of your organization gets killed, it's bad business to let the killer get away with it, bad all around, bad for every detective everywhere."*

Hearing Bogart's stirring words, I thought once again about Micah and his disappearance. The fact was I was not sure that he was dead, but my gut told me he was. In four years I had nothing to go on - no clue - to investigate in Micah's disappearance and that always bothered me I had done nothing in finding my best friend.

Thinking back to the list next to Craig Dale's book manuscript "The Daunting," I thought about the title to his book. An idea floated in my thinker that maybe Craig, in the course of doing the research for his book, had discovered something about Micah's disappearance - something that I had overlooked.

My mind was no longer focused on the Bogie and the Maltese Falcon. I went to my bookshelf and pulled out the latest edition of Webster's Dictionary and looked up the word "daunting."

I used my finger to scale down the page until I came across the word:

Daunting

: Tending to overwhelm or intimidate - a daunting task

Tending to overwhelm or intimidate? Now I was curious what Craig Dale's new book was about.

CHAPTER 6

After a wonderful dinner of Nickey's enchiladas, we settled into our Saturday night routine to watch "Starsky & Hutch" on ABC. I loved Starsky & Hutch - Nickey not so much. She watched it with me though, which told me once again how I hit the jackpot with this woman. The series was about two Southern California police detectives: David Michael Starsky played by Paul Michael Glaser, a dark-haired, Brooklyn transplant and U.S. Army veteran, with a streetwise manner and intense, sometimes childlike moodiness; and Kenneth Richard "Hutch" Hutchinson played by David Soul, the divorced, blond Duluth, Minnesota native with a more reserved and intellectual approach. Both actors were okay, but what I really liked about the show was that they were always tearing around and smoking their tires on the streets of some fake town named Bay City in California. The vehicle of choice was Starsky's two-door Ford Gran Torino, which was bright red with a large white vector stripe on both sides. That Gran Torino was the real star of the show.

During Starsky & Hutch and afterwards, when doing my nightly pushups and sit-ups, my mind kept drifting back to the mysterious list that was on Craig Dale's desk. So many questions I didn't have answers to. Where was Craig Dale? Besides Micah, who were the others on the list? Why were the dates important? Why Saturday? Why was my best friend's name on the list? Knowing the answers would not come to me tonight, I called it a night and went to bed. Nickey decided to stay up and watch the rest of "The Carol Burnett Show" on CBS.

After setting the clock for five a.m. my normal time to get up seven days a week, I crawled into bed and as my routine fell asleep in a matter of a couple of minutes.

Not sure when the dream started, but I was aware enough in my mind to know it was a dream. In the fog and mist of my dream, I was walking along a wilderness path that somehow felt familiar, but for some reason I could not recall where it was or if it had a name. It had a familiar feel about it is all I know. I knew it was autumn because the aspen leaves were in their full golden color and the wind was moving them, but there was no sound. I felt cold and close to freezing even though the sun was shining overhead with not one cloud in the sky. I walked for what seemed a long way down a winding path as I shivered from the cold. Then a crow landed in an evergreen right before me not ten feet away, and the crow's ebony black feathers glistened from the sunlight and the shadows as it jumped from limb to limb until it finally settled on a perch to watch me with intelligent eyes. From my Ute Indian heritage, I knew the crow was a powerful spirit, and they were all knowing in the spirit world. My Ute ancestors believed the crow knew all the mysteries of life and death. Sometimes they would appear and point you to a certain path that your life should follow. Sometimes they would show themselves foretelling of an impending death. As I was pondering the meaning of this crow, the crow twisted in an unusual way and looked directly below as did I following its gaze. Micah was now lying directly below the crow on his back, and his legs and arms were bent in an unnatural state telling me that Micah was dead. Micah my best friend was wearing the exact same clothes I had last seen him in the night before he disappeared. His eyes were closed and his black hair was dirty and full of leaves and twigs as if he had fallen. There was a trickle of blood still flowing from his ghostly pale lips. Micah looked dead, but if I had any doubt, there was a black handled Buck hunting knife I knew had a six inch blade, because I had one just like it.

The difference between the dream knife and my knife was in this dream the Buck knife was protruding from the center of his chest right where his heart was. Walking over, I kneeled down, and I touched the body of my friend as the crow stood on the tree limb above my head. Once I made contact with Micah's arm, I could feel the coldness of his flesh as if he never had lived. I touched Micah's arm once more as his body faded slowly until my best friend vanished right before my eyes. I stood and looked at the tree for the crow and realized the crow had vanished as well. Feeling a new presence behind me, I slowly turned and there was a man sitting on a rock ten feet away whittling a piece of aspen wood with a large Bowie knife. He was older than I was by at least thirty years but still seemed to have the grace of one much younger. The apparition was my height and weight and he looked like me - just older with shoulder length hair white as snow. The same apparition that had visited me twice before in my life. Although I had never seen a photograph of my grandfather since there was none, I knew this was he - the famous mountain man Matt Lee and the greatest foe the Ute Indians had ever faced – the one they called "Ghost" for his uncanny ability to fade into the Rocky Mountains after battling his ancient enemy. Grandfather stopped his whittling and looked directly into my soul as he spoke with a commanding and deep voice, "Dane, the tasks before you are simple enough and you already have the path to follow, for it leads to the mountains and the wilderness. Follow the sign and the tracks. Find out where your enemy is. Get after him as soon as you can. Strike him as hard as you can. Have no remorse, for he is evil, then move on."

My eyes snapped open, and I quickly sat up in bed as my heart seemed to want to pound out a hole in my chest. The room was pitch black except for the night light plugged into the outlet at the end of the bed that Nickey insisted on having me install. Reaching over, I touched Nickey as she lay peacefully sleeping with her back toward me as she was obviously content with the dreams she was having. Lying slowly back down on my sweat drenched pillow, I pondered the dream I just had. My feeling was that Micah's disappearance and Craig Dale's disappearance were somehow linked

Thinking through the details that were in my very lifelike dream, I knew that I had been given not only some truths but also a task to finish. One of the truths that presented itself in my dream I had already known and that was Micah was dead. Another truth was his death was not an accident just as once again this was nothing new to me since I had always known it by gut instinct. If the dream was true, then my best friend had been murdered by someone stabbing him in the heart. The other truth was that grandfather was showing me the path and the way as he did all men in the clan of Lee. I just had to interpret what grandfather was showing me.

Grandfather had said, *"Dane the task before you is simple enough and you already have the path to follow, for it leads to the mountains and the wilderness."* This made a lot of sense because Micah's 1970 Chevy pickup had been found in the Rocky Mountain National Park boundaries. I had also known Micah had been planning a trip there the day following after we had fished at Granby Lake.

I thought back to the exact words grandfather had also said, *"Follow the sign and the tracks."* I think he was talking about clues - the list of names and dates and possibly the book that Craig Dale was writing named "The Daunting."

Thinking hard and trying to remember grandfather's words before I forgot them, I rolled the last part around in my mind trying to find meaning in his words. I even mouthed the words a couple of times to make sure I could recollect them later when needed. Grandfather had said, *"Find out where your enemy is. Get after him as soon as you can. Strike him as hard as you can. Have no remorse, for he is evil, then move on."*

This last part baffled me because to the best of my knowledge, I had no enemies to think of. It would, of course, be difficult to locate and find my enemy if I didn't know I had one. Thinking hard on it, I thought maybe this enemy grandfather spoke of was not my enemy yet. Maybe he was telling me of future events. Almost laughing out loud, I thought, "I wish these damn Lee ghosts could be clearer in their meaning."

"Get after him as soon as you can. Strike him as hard as you can." Now what the hell did that mean? Arrest my enemy? Arrest them for what? In my mind, I knew the dream was the truth of

things that had happened and maybe of events that were going to happen, but it was still just a dream. Any course of action I took because of the dream of Micah and grandfather would just be speculation on my part. Anyone, including Nickey, who knew I acted because of this dream would think I was not right in my head. Hell, I was not even sure I was not off my rocker.

Bringing back grandfather's words again, I felt there was another truth - grandfather had said *"him"* and *"he"* which meant my enemy or future enemy was a male. I just didn't know who yet.

CHAPTER 7

Still thinking of the dream and of my grandfather, I looked at the clock on the bedside table and it was 3:35 in the morning. The dream was full of clues, and I also knew after the vivid dream and the visit from my grandfather, and with the thoughts now in my head, that there was no chance of going back to sleep. Slowly getting out of bed as not to disturb Nickey, I stood watching her sleep for a couple of minutes thanking the stars that Nickey was my woman.

Still in my underwear and T-shirt, I brewed a pot of coffee risking Nickey's wrath since she claimed her coffee was better than mine. After taking a sip to taste, once again, I realized that Nickey was spot on with her assessment of her coffee making ability over mine.

Still sipping on my bitter tasting coffee and wishing that Nickey would wake up and chew me out for making coffee in the first place, I then laughingly dumped my pot down the kitchen drain and made some good coffee. After I peeked into our bedroom, Nickey was still asleep, so I would have to suffer my brew for the first cup at least.

With a coffee cup in hand and after walking into the living room, I turned on the television and forgetting what time it was, I saw the black and white Indian head test pattern that stations used after their sign-off at the end of their broadcasting day buzzing on the screen. I realized it was too early for re-runs of Leave it to Beaver and the Andy Griffith show and knew that the Beaver, Wally, Andy, Barney, Otis, and my favorite television character of all time Ernest T. Bass, *"the best rock thrower in the county,"* would be on later.

Deciding that a little taste of music was my only option this early in the morning, I then walked to our dark walnut engraved television and stereo console to grab Waylon Jennings' new album "Are You Ready for the Country?" The first song was the same as the title of the album and had been written and recorded first by Neil Young, but I liked Waylon's version better. Turning the sound down low as not to disturb Nickey and trying to place the needle gently so not to scratch the album, I waited for the song I knew so well. *"Leftin' and a rightin' ain't a crime you know..."*

After Nickey woke up at 5 a.m., she took a quick shower and then walked into the kitchen wearing only her panties and a flimsy T-shirt, which caused me to burn my thumb as I lost my concentration on the breakfast while I was making bacon and eggs. I quickly put my thumb under the cold water faucet trying to soothe the burning sensation as Nickey laughed, swaying her bottom back and forth as she dumped out my coffee attempt of the morning. As I watched her obviously fine derriere as she started her ritual of making coffee, Nickey snickered once again as she said, "Dane, I am not even sure why you try to make coffee. It is a skill set you will never acquire."

I tried not to look at the almost naked woman in my kitchen so I would not burn myself a second time and finish the task of scrambling eggs. "Oh, I make better coffee than you Nickey Lynn; I tone down the fact to make you feel good."

She turned with that famous Nickey Lynn smirk and with her hip cocked to one side with her hand resting on it as she took notice of me scrambling eggs, "Is that so Mister!"

God, I loved this woman more than life itself. Dropping two pieces of wheat bread into the toaster, I said, "Mi Vida, could you grab two plates for the bacon and eggs?"

After grabbing the plates and setting them on the table, I scooped out some scrambled eggs onto the plates when Nickey said, "You must really like scrambled eggs since you make them all the time."

Chuckling to myself, I decided to finally tell her the truth. "Actually, I try to make an omelet every morning and once I try to flip it, then the eggs become scrambled."

I said this as she was starting to sit down, and she almost missed the chair while laughing that beautiful laugh of hers. After gaining her composure, she stated, "Next Saturday Mr. Lee, I will make you some Mexican omelets."

Sitting down in front of my plate of scrambled eggs, I sort of lost the desire to eat them thinking of future omelets. "Sounds wonderful Nickey! Next weekend you make the omelets and I will make the coffee."

With both elbows up on the table and her coffee cup just below her nose, Nickey breathed in the fresh-roasted aroma of her morning coffee. "Not on your life Mister."

It was decided as I knew it would be that it would be Grand Lake for fishing today so Nickey could spend time in those tourist traps in the Village of Grand Lake.

After quickly loading the county Blazer with our Wright & McGill fishing rods, Mitchell 300 fishing reels, salmon eggs, and enough Eagle Claw fishing tackle for the rest of eternity, we headed the fifteen miles north to Grand Lake.

While on the road, I took off my sweat stained Cattleman Crown Resistol cowboy hat and slapped on my beat to shit Denver Broncos fishing hat. The Broncos, after going 6 and 8 in 1975, still had John Ralston as the head coach. Nobody could guess how this year was going to go since the aging quarterback Charley Johnson had retired and the new starter behind the center was Steve Ramsey. So far this year they were 1 and 1 after losing the opener 17-7 against the Cincinnati Bengals at Riverfront stadium and bouncing back last week clobbering the New York Jets 46-13 at home in Denver at Mile High Stadium. Today at 2 p.m. at home again, they would play the Cleveland Browns. Nickey and I were hoping to be back to see the last half of the game.

After stopping for a spell to pitch fresh hay to Thunder and Cochise, we continued on to Grand Lake. I turned up the radio so

Nickey and I could sing along with the Bellamy Brothers and their song "Let Your Love Flow." *"When that love light shines all around us…"*

The day had turned into a pleasant day with above normal temperatures, and we drove with the windows down, letting the clear, crisp mountain air with the scent of pine and evergreen flow over us. As much as I wanted to enjoy the mountains, good music, and Mi Vida Nickey, my mind kept drifting back to the dream I had last night. I am sure grandfather was trying to show me the right path and the danger that the path might hold, but the more I rolled it around in my thinker, the more confused I got.

It was only a matter of a few minutes when we pulled into the outskirts of the Village of Grand Lake. Grand Lake was established about a 100 years prior at the elevation of 8,369 feet. The Village and town got its name from the lake on whose shores it was situated. The actual lake of Grand Lake is one of the largest natural bodies of water in Colorado. Grand Lake was originally an outfitting and supply point for the mining settlements of Lulu City, Teller City, and Gaskill. Today it is a tourist destination adjacent to the western entrance to Rocky Mountain National Park, which surrounds the lake and the town on three sides. In my mind the waters and the Village of Grand Lake were set in some of the most beautiful mountain country in the world.

After I parked the county Blazer on the north shore of the lake, Nickey did as she always did and walked the short distance to Grand Avenue which served as the main street of the town, and she let me fish by myself for a spell as she spent time browsing the tourist shops. After setting up my rod and reels, I cast two rods into the cool water of the lake and then placed them on rod holders as I sat down in one of two lawn chairs I always carried in the back of the Blazer.

Now with Nickey off doing her happy thing and having some time to myself again, I started to concentrate once again on the meaning of my dream last night. I remembered the words that grandfather had spoken in the dream. *"Dane the task before you is simple enough and you already have the path to follow, for it leads to the mountains and the wilderness. Follow the sign and the tracks. Find out where your enemy is. Get after him as soon as you can. Strike him as hard as you can. Have no remorse, for he is evil, then move on."*

After pondering for a spell on grandfather's words, *"Dane the tasks before you are simple enough and you already have the path to follow,"* it was obvious grandfather felt I already had the clues needed to locate my enemy or my future enemy. The list with Micah's name and the date he disappeared, along with the other dates and names, was the biggest clue. How Craig Dale compiled the list I did not know, and so far he had not shown up as yet to ask him about it. I started to think Mr. Dale's book that he is writing titled "The Daunting" was also a big clue. It might not be proper or even legal at this point, but my gut was telling me I needed to look at that manuscript

CHAPTER 8

After Nickey had satisfied her Grand Lake tourist shop addiction for now, she returned with a small bag of do-dads and a novel she had purchased. Between the two of us that day, we caught four rainbow and two brown trout with each one being safely released back into the cool water of the lake.

As Nickey and I fished the day away, the temperature started to drop before noon and some dark clouds rolled in from the north as a storm was brewing above the white snowcapped peaks in Rocky Mountain National Park. As the day grew long in hours and on the western side of the lake just below the horizon, an eerie mist started to form. The feathery haze chilled the air as it ghosted its way from west to east swallowing up boaters and fishermen alike. Watching the mist reminded me that my ancestors, the Grand River Utes, had a different name for this lake; they called it Spirit Lake.

Even though Nickey had heard the tale from me before, I once again told her why the Utes called it Spirit Lake. It was a tale told from all the clan of Lee grandfathers to their grandchildren. My grandfather - my dad's dad - told me and Micah this antique tale for the first time one evening around a campfire on the east side of

Grand Lake in the moon shadow at the base of Bald Mountain. Clearing my voice, *"One summer evening long ago a thunderstorm rolled in and over the Never Summer Mountains when a small band of Utes was camping on the shores of Grand Lake. In the midst of the storm, a war party of their ancient enemies of the Arapahoe and Cheyenne attacked the Ute Indians. As the storm raged, so did the battle; the Ute warriors loaded all the women, children, and elderly in their rafts and set them adrift on the lake for their safety. Numerous warriors had fallen in the battle on both sides, but the Utes drove off the attacking tribes and were victorious in the battle. The chief of the Utes at that time looked to the white-capped lake and saw the rafts had capsized during the storm and all the women, children, and the elderly could not be seen. After a night of grieving for their dead, the next night it was said the Ute warriors could see across the now calm waters the spirits of the dead families rising in the mist. The Ute chief and these warriors that had fought so hard to protect their loved ones were so shaken by seeing the spirits that they never returned to Spirit Lake again."*

As I stared across at the mist that had formed on the lake, I could almost feel my ancestors calling out from across the ancient passages of time with a mournful cry. It was times like this I could feel the Ute blood as it rushed within my veins. With the fishing done for the day, it was time to head back to Granby. Looking at the woman I loved as we started up the Blazer, I knew she would never fully understand the connection I had with the Rocky Mountains - my spirit and my ancestors' spirits were part of the energy that flowed here. The Rocky Mountains were engraved within my soul. It was an Indian thing. My Ute blood had thinned through the years starting when my grandmother Walk With Ghost had married Matt Lee. I still had enough of the Ute Indian blood in me to feel my connection to these mountains of old. Just as I was proud of my dad and all my mountain men grandfathers before me, I was as equally proud of my Ute Indian heritage.

Pulling onto Highway 34 heading south, I watched Nickey reading her new book she had bought in Grand Lake called "Centennial" by James Michener. Since it occupied Nickey, my mind wandered to the disappearance of Craig Dale again and his unfinished book "The Daunting." Since Mr. Dale was not officially reported missing, I was not sure of the legal aspect of starting an investigation. I would have to sit down with Sheriff Walker tomorrow and go over the particulars of what happened yesterday regarding the welfare check at Craig Dale Wilderness Photography business.

Nickey and I made it home early to Granby just in time for the Broncos and Browns game. After adjusting the rabbit ear antennae and getting the tin foil we used for better reception in just the right spot, we watched the Broncos blow out the Cleveland Browns 44-13 at Mile High Stadium. It was a game for the record books, and I was glad we could watch it as Rick Upchurch tied an NFL record by returning two punts for touchdowns.

It had been an uneventful and quiet day and after the Broncos and Browns game, Nickey and I grilled up a couple of burgers and then we hit the sack for an early night. Nickey once again became absorbed reading her novel Centennial, and I quickly fell asleep.

The night was peaceful without Micah or my grandfather returning with more clues or visions of the past or present. I guess they felt I had enough clues and information to act on. I just didn't really know where to start.

Waking up at 5 a.m. I once again slipped out of bed so as not to disturb Nickey since she had the day off. After watching Nickey sleep for several minutes, I headed into the kitchen to heat the now day old coffee that Nickey had made, knowing full well it would still be better than anything that I could brew. After toasting two blueberry pop tarts, I then tried to wash them down with a glass of orange Tang. After drinking half the glass, I looked at the remaining orange mixture left in the glass and wondered why the hell I ever drank this stuff. Shaking my head thinking if it was good enough for John Glenn and the rest of the astronauts at NASA, it was good enough for me, so I grimaced and slammed the remaining Tang even though it tasted like shit.

Knowing Nickey would see to Thunder's and Cochise's care and feeding since she did not have to work, I headed out the door at 6 in the morning.

Sitting in the Blazer for a few minutes to let it warm up, I watched the moon disappear as it arced downward in the western horizon as the new sun of the day started its daily arc in the eastern horizon. The sky had cleared during the night and not one cloud was visible as far as I could see. In my side mirror, I could see the ghostly vapor of the hot exhaust as it met the morning cool air. Autumn was now in full swing as the aspens' leaves that dotted the surrounding mountains were now in their full golden color. It would not be long before old man winter would once again bring its below freezing cold and snow to my Rocky Mountains and my front doorstep.

Feeling the interior of the Blazer warming up, I shifted into reverse and backed out, making my way to Agate Avenue and Highway 40 and pointed the Blazer west. Once I got to 2nd and Agate, I pulled over in front of Craig Dale Wilderness Photography and with the engine still running, I studied the building for a few minutes, and I determined it looked just like it had when Nickey and I left it on Saturday. It would seem that Craig had yet to return. As I looked up at the 2nd floor window where Mr. Dale was writing his book "The Daunting" and what used to be Micah's living room, nostalgia overcame me as I remembered more than a few nights I had slept on Micah's couch that used to sit just below that window. Too many times to count after having a few more beers than I should have, I fell asleep watching the Denver Broncos or the Denver Rockets. I always wondered what Micah would have thought about his favorite basketball team the Rockets later changing their name to the Denver Nuggets after he had gone missing. With a huge sigh and after taking one last glimpse, I shifted into 2nd gear and let out slowly on the clutch and pulled back on Agate Avenue, continuing on toward Hot Sulphur Springs and the sheriff's office.

Sheriff Walker's county issued Blazer was in the parking lot as I drove in. Thinking no time was better than the present, I decided to talk to him this morning first thing about Craig Dale. Walking down the hallway, I stopped in front of Micah's missing person flyer, and I took my forefinger and the finger next to it and pressed Micah's photo for several seconds hoping for a flash of insight from either Micah or my grandfather. Nothing happened, of course, and I felt sort of foolish in doing so. Under my breath so no one could hear as I looked at the old photo of my missing best friend, I said, "I have not forgotten you."

Sheriff Walker's office door was open as always and he was busy looking over some reports on his desk. He had not noticed me yet, and I stood in the doorway for a minute thinking about my boss. Tom Walker was in his late 50s and was one of my dad's best friends; he was the one who talked me into joining the sheriff's office. Tom was a decent and good man who was a part-time pastor at his church. His wife had passed away a year ago from cancer down in Denver, and he had lost his only child and son in a rollover crash on top of Trail Ridge Road in Rocky Mountain National Park ten years ago. Tom's hair had gotten thinner and now was all gray. He was still a stout man at 6' tall and 190 pounds and kept himself in shape. He had been the sheriff here in Grand County as long as I could remember.

Tom's eyes lifted off the page, and he was a bit startled when he finally saw me. "Dane, you got to quit sneaking up on us elderly. Come in and grab a chair."

I started at the beginning of when I was told by the dispatcher about Grand Lake Plumbing and their concern for the well-being of Craig Dale after his no-show after calling in with no heat. I walked Sheriff Walker through Nickey and me entering the building and what we had found. He was not pleased when I said if Mr. Dale did not pay the bill in getting the heat going, I promised Frank the owner of Grand Lake Plumbing that the county would pick up the tab. Tom was relieved somewhat when I told him it was a minor wiring problem with a circulation pump. I also showed him the list of names I had written and that Micah's name was at the bottom of the list. He, of course, knew the story of Micah's disappearance.

Sheriff Walker listened with interest as I told him the story. He spun a Bic pen around in between his thumb and forefinger. After I had spoken out loud, I knew it sounded as if I was making a mountain out of a molehill. I did not tell the sheriff of my dream of seeing Micah dead with a Buck knife in his chest or of what my grandfather had mentioned in my dream about my enemy.

Setting the pen down on top of his desk, Tom leaned forward and looked me in the eye and asked, "Is that it Dane? Am I missing something here other than Micah's name being on the list?"

I shook my head "no" realizing it did in fact sound as if I was looking for things that were not there. The dream and my gut instinct told me differently, but there was no way that the sheriff would allow any type of investigation on a dream and a feeling.

Speaking quietly and feeling slightly foolish, "Yes, that about sums it up, sheriff."

Sheriff Walker now placed his forearms on top of his desk as he spoke in the commanding voice he had. "First off you did the right thing following up on Grand Lake Plumbing's concern, and I hope you put the keys right back where you found them. The second thing, we are not in the business of paying for plumbing repairs, so in the future restrain yourself from obligating the county for such repairs. The third thing is that no one has reported Mr. Dale missing and for all we know, he is down in Denver on some drunken binge which is his business and not ours. As for Micah's name being on the list, you can ask Mr. Dale about that when he returns to Granby and Grand County. So summing it all up Dane, right now Mr. Dale is not considered missing in the eyes of the law and as far as we know, no crime has been committed. So, until something changes you need to go about your duties you do so well, but for now you need to stay away from Craig Dale Wilderness Photography."

CHAPTER 9

I knew full well that Sheriff Walker was right in saying what he did given the information available at this time, but my gut told me differently, and I knew Mr. Dale just like Micah was never coming back to his home and place of business on Agate Avenue. I had to sit on my thumbs in this regard until someone reported him missing.

Taking the list I had copied at Craig Dale's, I pinned it to the bulletin board next to my desk.

Samael Amos
Bryan Amen 9/27/1975 SATURDAY
Jerry Toney 10/5/1974 SATURDAY
Randy Weems 9/8/1973 SATURDAY
Shawn Lord 10/13/1973 SATURDAY
Kevin Kyriss 10/21/1972 SATURDAY
Micah Trask 9/16/1972 SATURDAY

Each time I looked up from doing paperwork, my eyes would cross the list and linger for a spell wondering what it meant.

The rest of the week went by ploddingly. Each and every time I went out and about doing my routine and my job, I drove by the building on 191 E Agate Avenue numerous times during the course of my duties. Several times I would stop the Blazer in front and get out and knock on the door knowing already that no one was home. The building remained silent and abandoned. Touching the glass on the front door, I could feel the heat inside the building radiating to the outside. It would seem that the service plumber had done his job, and the heat remained running despite knowing that not a living soul would take comfort in it. At each of the visits to the front door of Craig Dale Wilderness Photography, I would look at the whiskey barrel flower planter that had Micah's old key hidden beneath it and I had to restrain myself from using it. I knew that there was another clue to the disappearance of Micah Trask in the manuscript "The Daunting" sitting on Craig Dale's desk. I just knew it. Each time I bent to remove the key, Sheriff Walker's words rambled through my mind, "For now you need to stay away from Craig Dale Wilderness Photography."

On Friday, winter briefly kicked autumn to the curb, and it snowed a couple of inches in the morning, causing several wrecks on Highway 40 and one rollover on Highway 34 due to icy conditions. Our department and the state patrol were busy dealing with the aftermath of these wrecks the entire day.

Saturday saw another loss for the hometown Middle Park Panthers as they stumbled to a record of 2 and 2 against Denver Lutheran down in Denver although it was a close game that put Purple Panther Pride on the losing end 21 to 20. Nickey and I both had to work and missed the game.

Nickey and I went about living our lives with our jobs and each other, and if not for my brooding over the possibility of Craig Dale missing and the haunting list of names, life would have been wonderful. My love for Mi Vida Nickey could not be stronger, but my mind was always drifting back to the list and the manuscript "The Daunting," and she felt my uneasiness.

September had come and gone, and now it was the beginning of October and the Rocky Mountains proved once again that the weather had a mind of its own the closer you got to the heavens. After a pleasant snowfall on Friday followed by bone chilling cold on Saturday, the sun found its way back on Sunday and brought a lovely day with it. With not a cloud in the sky and the blue stretching as far as the eye could see, what was left of the snow melted and most of the white powder was gone by 10 a.m.

Nickey and I decided it was a good day to ride Thunder and Cochise, and we spent the rest of Sunday morning enjoying our horses and each other. After a good ride and stretch for the horses, Nickey Lynn and I made love in the tack room. During our lovemaking was the only time that my mind was not preoccupied with the mysterious list of names and Craig Dale's manuscript "The Daunting."

After fixing a flat tire on the two horse trailer I used to haul the horses to Rocky Mountain National Park, Nickey and I hurried home to watch the Denver Broncos.

Heading home, I slipped in an audio cassette - Eagles Greatest Hits (1971–1975), and the song "One of These Nights" written by Henley and Frey burst through the Jensen speakers mounted in the door of the Blazer. As Henley's smooth voice brought the song to life, Nickey closed her eyes and swayed and mouthed the words. *"One of these nights..."*

There was a stanza in the song that stood out to me with everything that was going on with Micah's and Craig Dale's disappearances. Even though the song did not pertain to my demons that now haunted me, the words *"You got your demons"* and *"Well, I got a few of my own"* served up flashes of memories of Micah and me growing up. There was no doubt Micah's disappearance and not knowing what happened to him was my demon - my cross to bear.

Nickey and I walked into the house at exactly 2 pm as the game at Mile High Stadium was starting between the Broncos and the San Diego Chargers. Dan Fouts the Chargers starting quarterback vs the Broncos starting quarterback Steve Ramsey. It was no contest as once again Rick Upchurch of the Broncos in the second quarter ran back a punt for a 92 yard touchdown. Jim Turner of the Broncos kicked four field goals, and running back Lonnie Perrin ran from the one yard line and scored the game's lone offensive touchdown. My favorite running back Otis Armstrong led the Broncos with 91 yards rushing. The final score was 26 - 0 which put the Broncos' record at 3 and 1 for the year to date. Even though I watched the game for the entire four quarters, I did not really see the game as my mind drifted once again to the cryptic list with Micah's name on it. I only reacted when the Broncos scored because Nickey started her fist pumping and as her routine when the Broncos were winning, she would start her "Whoop, whoop" as her smile stretched ear to ear.

After the Bronco victory Nickey served up beef and bean burritos with her famous green chili she makes in the crock pot and as we were sitting at the kitchen table, she finally set her fork down and said, "Okay Dane, all week you have been zoned out and have barely talked at all. I understand your mind is still searching for answers about Micah, and this business of Craig Dale gone missing has triggered painful memories. So in the morning I am going to make some phone calls about the names on the list that Craig Dale had. Sheriff Walker told you not to go near Craig Dale Wilderness Photography, but he never told me that. We need to do something before you go crazy and take me along with you."

Setting down my fork, I looked across the table to Mi Vida and realized she was the woman I always needed in my life. She knows me better than I know myself. She was right; I had to do something even if it was the wrong thing. It was starting to eat me alive. Reaching across and gingerly grabbing Nickey's hand to hold when I spoke, "You know Nickey, I love you very much and you are right; I need to do something and it honors me you want to help. When at work tomorrow if you can start checking on those names, I will go back to Craig Dale's when I have time and take a quick gander at "The Daunting" manuscript. There has to be a clue or clues in it as well."

Nickey stood up and bent over the small table and kissed me full on the lips. After stepping back and with the cutest smile and glistening eyes, she said, "Now we got that settled, let's go watch Sonny and Cher and then Kojack!"

Nickey fell asleep quickly after watching our shows. I worked out and did my sit-ups, pushups and a little weight lifting before bed, but once I lay down, a good night's sleep was hard to come by. I was excited to delve into the manuscript, but it made me a little nervy going against the sheriff's wishes.

After falling asleep, grandfather entered my dreams on the same familiar wilderness trail from my last dream, but this time Micah's body was not visible although I could feel his presence in the dream. Grandfather was there and still whittling a piece of aspen wood with a large Bowie knife. Once again, grandfather stopped his whittling and looked directly into my soul as he spoke with a commanding and deep voice and said the exact phrase word for word as he said before, *"Dane, the tasks before you are simple enough and you already have the path to follow, for it leads to the mountains and the wilderness. Follow the sign and the tracks. Find out where your enemy is. Get after him as soon as you can. Strike him as hard as you can. Have no remorse, for he is evil, then move on."*

CHAPTER 10

Nickey and I both left the house at the same time in the morning at 6 a.m. but in different directions. It was Nickey's morning again to see to Thunder and Cochise, and I was going to make a quick stop at Craig Dale Wilderness Photography. On the way to the sheriff's office in Hot Sulphur Springs, I stopped once again in front of the building at 191 E Agate Ave.

I stepped out of the already warm and heated county issued Blazer into the cold of an early October morning. The sun was still a ways from peeking over the mountains to the east, but the stars had already started to fade in the early morning sky, and clouds were riding the wind from the north, and it would not be long before the stars would be completely covered and tucked in for the day. The north wind had come up during the night and once I stepped up on the curb, I was hit in the face by an aspen leaf as it was carried on a chilled gust of wind. It stuck momentarily between my nose and right eye before another cold puff of air dislodged it, and the decayed leaf caught the air current and rode it, I am sure, looking for its final resting place for the season.

Once I got my eyes adjusted to the early morning light, I looked for a full minute at the window on the second floor and could not detect any light whatsoever in the building. It looked abandoned still, and my gut feeling is that it was. Taking my flashlight and turning it on, I looked through the glass on the front door, and the interior looked just as it did the day that Nickey and I had entered looking for Mr. Dale. Taking off my right glove, I touched the glass and once again I could feel the heat from inside the building. Looking down at the half whiskey flower barrel hiding Micah's key, I decided it was not the time to enter the building since I needed to start my day at the office first.

Once back inside the Blazer and feeling the warmth of the heater, I took a moment and thought about my dream last night and grandfather. The wilderness trail in the dream each time felt familiar, but I could not put a name to it. I felt as if I had been on the trail many times before, but in the dream I was always concentrating on what grandfather was saying and not on the trail itself. My gut was telling me that the dream wilderness trail was not just a random trail - that it was more than that. It was another clue to the mystery surrounding Micah's disappearance.

After looking at my wristwatch and realizing I had spent more time here than I should, I pulled out onto the empty road and headed west toward the office. Sorting through my cassette case, I located Creedence Clearwater Revival's "Chronicle, Volume 1." John Fogerty's band was a favorite of mine. Punching in the cassette, I was happy to find that the tape had already been played to the fourth song which was "Bad Moon Rising." Turning up the volume, realizing there was nothing finer in this world than loud music and open highway, I sang along as if I was part of the band as the Blazer headed west. *"I see trouble on the way..."*

Pulling into the parking lot, I took notice that Sheriff Walker's Blazer was not there and then I remembered it was his day off today, which was a good thing since I was going to go against his orders and start looking into Craig Dale's disappearance. The only vehicles present were the two jailers, Yvonne the dispatcher, and the county Blazer driven by Officer Gene Sanford. Nickey Lynn would be along shortly.

Walking past the missing posters that were posted, I stopped as was my habit and looked at Micah's poster and once again pressed my fingers on my best friend's photo hoping for some new insight into his vanishing. I felt nothing - no flash of understanding or clarity. All I could feel was the old photo paper just like every time in the last four years. The feeling of dread and hopelessness flooded over me. Closing my eyes, I gathered in the sense of hopelessness; I wanted to feel it in every fiber of my being because I needed to use it. Turning to face the feeling and make it my quest once again, I turned the feeling of hopelessness into a weapon - something to use to motivate me. The disappearance of Craig Dale and the grandfather dreams had given me something to go on. The instinct of the Lee mountain men had been reawakened, and I had to go with that. No one would understand, but that didn't matter - I understood. Taking my fingers from the photo, I whispered, "Soon my friend I will have the answers I seek."

Sitting down at my desk, I looked at a few memos that had been placed there by the night shift. Most were about traffic stops and one which resulted in a drunk driving arrest. I had just finished reading the last one when Gene Sanford pulled up a spare chair and sat down next to my desk setting the book "Rocky Mountain Ghost" on my desk. I looked at the book first and then at Gene with his ear-to-ear smile when he finally said, "Finished this last night and I could hardly put it down. You probably already know this Dane, but your Grandpa Matt Lee was a real badass. After a band of warriors attacked him and some of his mountain man buddies when they discovered the La Caverna Del Oro - the lost Spanish gold cavern - he was the sole survivor of the battle. And according to the book he was then possessed by a ghost or a demon from the cave and then for the next two years he took on the whole Ute Indian nation killing a shit load of their best warriors, and then he would hack off one of their ears to mark them. Great stuff in that book, and I hope someone makes it into a movie."

Nickey had pulled up a chair as well after she had entered the office and was listening with apt attention as Gene was giving his two thumbs up review of the book about my grandfather. Nickey sort of wrinkled up her nose after hearing about the hacking off of the ears. Nickey looked at me as if I had chopped off the ears of those long dead Indians instead of my grandfather; then she looked back at Gene. "What did he do with the ears after he cut them off?"

Gene scooted up in his chair and put his arms on my desk as he was visibly excited about retelling the story in Gene fashion. "He kept them in a leather pouch like trophies until he got all lovey-dovey with Dane's grandmother. Once he hooked up with his lady, he got all sorts of pacifying and buried them in the woods. Once he was done with that, the demon or ghost seemed happy I guess and he left Grandpa Matt alone. Then all was good for like twenty or thirty years until some snot-nosed cavalry dudes shot grandma Walk With Ghost in Grand Lake after one tried kissing her and she scratched up his face something horrible. Then Grandpa Matt went on a killing spree and killed a shit load of these army punks for almost killing grandma. This is a great book and has a federal marshal named Eric Robert and another badass bounty hunter named Doug Webb. Oh yeah, there is this rocking man-killing horse as well named Cimarron in the book. What a great read! You both need to read this book. I wonder if it is all true. Is it all true, Dane?"

Nickey had grabbed the book and flipped it over to read the description on the book before she said, "I might have to quit reading the book I am on now and read this one first. Sounds good with a lot of action and adventure. And a good western love story as well."

Gene chuckled then added after Nickey quit speaking, "You will love it Nickey since you are living with Grandpa Matt's grandson mountain man Dane Lee."

Gene, after stating the obvious about Nickey's and my living arrangements, asked me again, "Dane, do you know if this story is true?"

Reaching out so Nickey would hand me the book about my grandfather, I turned it over several times looking at the winter scene photo on the cover and the back with the blue moon overhead which made me think of Craig Dale Wilderness Photography. Gene was waiting patiently for an answer so I said, "What you described Gene, about my grandfather and grandmother in the book seems to be close to what had always been told to me about them by my dad and his dad. There was no doubt to have lived back in those days you had to be a badass. By all of family accounting, Grandfather Matt was that and much more. Guess I will have to read the book myself."

I looked at the book and wondered how the writer had gotten his information since he had not interviewed me nor my dad for the book. We were the last of the Lee clan and unless I had children, the seed of the Lee mountain men would die with me. As I was pondering the demise of the Lee mountain men, Gene asked in a somewhat confused voice, "How do you know Bryan Amen?"

I looked up from the book to Gene as he was not looking at me, but past me. In an even more confused tone of voice I asked, "What did you say?"

Gene was still looking past me and said, "Bryan Amen, do you know him?"

Nickey was the first one to catch on as she had followed Gene's gaze. "The list Dane! The list that Craig Dale wrote!"

I shook my head because I was still not following as I looked at Nickey as she was looking past me and behind me. Now following her gaze, I turned and saw what they saw. The list I had copied from Craig Dale's desk and had pinned to my bulletin board had Bryan Amen's name listed second.

CHAPTER 11

Reaching over, I unpinned the list from my bulletin board and then handed it to Gene for him to look at before I asked, "Do you know Bryan Amen?"

Gene took the list and looked again at it and read it again before he said, "Of course I know Bryan. He dated my sister until about a year ago or so. He used to live in Tabernash right off of Red Dirt Hill. Nice enough guy - a real he-man, macho type just like you Dane. Spends all of his free time up in Rocky Mountain National Park rock climbing. Real nature and mountain man dude. I was kind of bummed when my sister and he broke up. Do you know him, Dane?"

Nickey jumped in and answered for me. "No Gene, neither Dane nor I know Bryan. Do you know how we can get in touch with him? We would like to ask him some questions."

Gene shook his head "no" before he spoke again. "My sister and he had a huge fight about a year ago and one weekend he left without ever speaking to her again. My sister was heartbroken and did not think the fight was enough to break them up, but obviously Bryan thought differently. She believed he moved back down to Denver where he was from. As far as I know, she had not talked to him since. Why all this interest in Bryan?"

Leaning forward with my arms on my desk and pondering what Gene had just told Nickey and I about Bryan Amen, I said, "It might be nothing, but Bryan's name was on a list that we found in Craig Dale's place. The last name on the list is Micah Trask, and he was my best friend growing up. I know you don't know Micah since you moved here to Grand County two years ago."

Gene looked at me as he took in everything I said and then he replied, "Micah Trask? He is the guy on the missing poster you look at every day isn't he?"

Nodding my head up and down in a "yes" motion, "One and the same, Gene. Micah has been missing for over four years now. They found Micha's Ford F-250 parked off of Trail Ridge Road in the park next to Phantom Creek. He never came back for it and has been missing ever since. Besides Bryan's name, do you recognize any of the other names? And the date after Bryan's name does that mean anything to you?"

Gene read the list once more and then handed it back before speaking. "Nope on both accounts other than the date behind Bryan's name would be close to the time my sister and he broke up."

Taking the piece of paper back with the mysterious list on it, I locked eyes with Nickey for a second and I could see that she was as baffled as I was. Looking back toward Gene, I gave him a task. "Gene, today when you have time, get a hold of your sister and try to get a phone number or address for Bryan. I would like to call him and chat with him about this list and see if maybe he knows what it is about."

Gene acknowledged that he would contact his sister, but it was still too early to call her, so he made ready and left to start his patrol. Nickey looked at me for a couple of seconds before she said, "How weird is that?"

Letting it roll around in my brain pan for a minute, I said, "Maybe not so weird Nickey, and it could mean absolutely nothing. Here, take the list and you can make some phone calls before you go out on patrol. I will head back to Granby and take a gander at Craig Dale Wilderness Photography."

Stepping out of the office, I had to pull up the collar of my coat to cover my ears as the unkind wind was still gusting out of the north. The sun had finally peaked above the mountain tops in the east, but the warmth from the sun was having little or no effect since the sky was full of dark and dreary clouds with the hint of an October snow in them.

Pulling out onto Highway 40 and pointing the nose of the Blazer east, I pondered what Gene had said about his sister's old boyfriend Bryan. As much as I tried to connect the dots between Bryan and Micah, I could find nothing substantial. The only similarity was that both Micah and Bryan were nature lovers and mountain men types and had spent considerable time up in Rocky Mountain National Park, which meant diddly squat, for most people in Grand County spent considerable time there and most were nature lovers. You did not live in the Rocky Mountains unless you loved the outdoors.

About halfway in between Granby and the office, the police radio crackled, "Undersheriff Lee, this is dispatch."

Reaching down, I unhooked the microphone from its holder on the side of the radio and lost the grip and fumbled it as the microphone sprang and bounced over onto the passenger side floorboard. Grabbing the black coiled cord, I pulled the microphone closer until I could reach down and pick it up without crashing the Blazer. Once I had it under control, I keyed the transmit button. "Dispatch, this is Dane."

The radio remained silent for about thirty seconds as I could visualize Yvonne sipping on her coffee cup. Finally, the radio crackled again, "Dane I just got off the phone with a woman from Belle Fourche, South Dakota named Patty Dale. She is the sister of Craig Dale the nature photographer on Agate Avenue in Granby. She said that she had not heard from her brother for several weeks and he had always been good about calling every other Sunday. She is concerned and would like someone to check on Mr. Dale to see if he is okay."

Well, that made it official what I was going to do anyway. Keying the microphone once again, "Heading there now, Yvonne. Would you please type up everything you just told me in a memo and log the time of the call from Miss Dale and lay that on Sheriff Walker's desk so he can see it first thing tomorrow morning when he gets in. I want to keep him updated on this."

Pulling up in front of Craig Dale's business and home, I never even hesitated this time and went straight to the whiskey half barrel flower planter and tilted it back far enough to expose Micah's long ago hidden key. Taking the key, I knocked loudly on the front door and waited a minute and when there was no answer, I inserted the key and turned it until the deadbolt snapped back into the door with a solid thud.

Opening the door slowly, I stepped in and the heat from the interior felt better than the cold from the north wind outside. Looking and not finding the light switch, then remembering it was to the right of the front door, I flipped it on and the overhead lights came to life. The front entrance and this room looked exactly the same since Nickey and I were last here. No one including Mr. Dale had been here in between then and now. Speaking in a loud and clear voice, "Mr. Dale this is the Grand County Sheriff's office checking on you in case you might need some sort of assistance."

The building remained silent and brooding except for the slight rattle of the windows from the north wind. Walking slowly and cautiously across the room to the rear of the building and the stairs that led to the apartment above, I felt uneasy. I guess it was because now knowing Craig Dale had been officially reported as having no contact with anyone, including family, I knew he had gone missing just like my best friend Micah. Reaching the bottom of the stairs, I had the feeling of having just walked over Craig Dale's grave. My gut instinct told me that Mr. Dale was not only missing, but he was also no longer among the living. I did not need a dream of Mr. Dale with a Buck knife protruding from his chest to show me that - I just knew.

Looking up the stairs into the darkness, I found the light switch on the left on the exterior wall and flipped it on, and the overhead light at the top of the stairs snapped on. Knowing the building was empty, but feeling the need to announce myself, I said in a loud and clear voice once again, "Mr. Dale, this is Dane Lee from the Grand County Sheriff's office, and I am here to check up on you. Your sister Patty called, and she is worried about you. I am coming up the stairs now."

There was no sneaking up the stairs even if I wanted to. Each step creaked and moaned when I shifted my weight onto it. Once I reached the top of the stairs, I turned on the light switch once again, and several table lamps lit up. Standing there for a few seconds, I surveyed the room and everything was how I remembered it from Nickey's and my visit from last time. The room was warm, but not too hot and I took off my coat and laid it on the couch.

Moving over to Craig Dale's desk, I pulled out the chair and sat down. Everything looked the same except for a slight coating of dust that had gathered on the yellow Smith Corona electric typewriter. Next to the Smith Corona as before was a stack of about 200 double spaced typewritten pages with a cover sheet stating the name of his book "The Daunting" by Craig Dale. And to the left of the stack of papers was the list once again.

Samael Amos
Bryan Amen 9/27/1975 SATURDAY
Jerry Toney 10/5/1974 SATURDAY
Randy Weems 9/8/1973 SATURDAY
Shawn Lord 10/13/1973 SATURDAY
Kevin Kyriss 10/21/1972 SATURDAY
Micah Trask 9/16/1972 SATURDAY

Not wanting to touch anything in case this building might become a crime scene, I grabbed a pencil from the cup holder next to the typewriter and using the eraser, I carefully moved the cover sheet over to the left off of the stack of papers so it covered the mysterious list of names.

The first line of "The Daunting" manuscript was a question, and I had to read it twice because I was stunned at what it said. *"Have you ever had someone you know or loved that has disappeared in Rocky Mountain National Park in the remote mountains of Colorado?"*

CHAPTER 12

The first couple of sentences told me that "The Daunting" was a non-fiction book instead of fiction. The next several hours passed quickly as I skimmed the double-spaced pages. I felt somewhat guilty, reading what was obviously an unfinished manuscript with numerous spelling and grammar errors; nevertheless, I was captivated by the words that Mr. Dale had typed. It would seem that Craig Dale was not only a fantastic nature photographer, but he also had a flair and a knack for investigative work and reading his words, I felt I got to know the man himself as his personality came forth in his writing. Craig Dale, by his subject alone, was a man of the wilderness and mountains such as Micah and me. Craig also seemed to be a no nonsense man who saw the world in the exact terms as if only in black and white with no gray areas.

The first couple of chapters told me what his book "The Daunting" was about and his attempts to find answers to his questions. For whatever reason Mr. Dale had become interested in people that had gone missing in Rocky Mountain National Park and he had tried to document the ongoing disappearances in this yet unfinished book. Some of what I read was not new to me or anyone that lived or had lived in Grand County, for these mountains had often claimed the lives of those not prepared for the high wilderness and mountain frontier. What was astonishing was not that folks go missing in the remote wilderness, but how frequently it actually happened according to Mr. Dale's findings in this manuscript.

It would seem that people had been disappearing under mysterious and not so mysterious circumstances in Rocky Mountain National Park before and since the state of Colorado kept any records of this type dating all the way back to the 1940's, not to mention those that had disappeared in those remote mountains before the record keeping.

The next couple of chapters of "The Daunting" dealt with trappers, mountain men, and Indians in the mid to late 19th century. I quickly skimmed these chapters because this seemed like nothing unusual to me since my Grandfather Matt Lee himself had killed over twenty Ute Indians in his bid for revenge in his declared war against the Ute nations in the 1840's.

The next couple of chapters dealt with children that had gone missing within the park boundaries like Dusty and Rusty Hines – eleven year old twin boys that had wandered away from their Boy Scout troop in 1957 in the Moraine Park area. Search and rescue and over 1000 volunteers combed the area where the boys went missing for over ten days. Their bodies or their remains have never been located even until this day.

There was also an account of one I remembered from back when I was a freshman in high school when two Middle Park High School seniors disappeared. Tim Jensen the football quarterback and Denise Reed one of the Middle Park cheerleaders who were boyfriend and girlfriend skipped school one autumn day to do some remote mountain hiking never to be heard from again.

There were many other cases documented in the book and more than I thought possible just got a passing mention of their disappearances. Almost all of the cases mentioned in the book of missing children that were never found I had never heard of even though I had lived in Grand County all my life. It amazed me and it astonished me at Mr. Dale's ability to find all this information.

The next four chapters were about folks unprepared for the adverse weather that can occur up in the park, especially above timberline. Most of the folks depicted in these chapters were out-of-staters and flatlanders that decided to take a nature hike in the autumn months not dressed for the fast changing weather and not knowing of the danger they put themselves in. One such example was a 46-year-old father, Mark Robinson and his 23-year-old son Tommy Robinson, who both were from Kansas and had decided to hike the Alpine Ridge Trail while vacationing in Colorado. This trail was for experienced hikers only and reached some lofty heights almost 2000 feet above timberline. On October 15th in 1970 wearing only shorts and T-shirts, they left their truck parked on the side of the road at 11 in the morning. The temperature according to the documentation in Mr. Dale's book was in the mid-50's and sunny. October 15th in 1970 also was the first snowfall that later that afternoon dumped over two feet of heavy wet snow and would cause the closing of Trail Ridge Road for the season. The Robinsons were never heard from again.

The book told the same sad tale time and time again of those that went to the park for a vacation or just a drive in the mountains for the day and simply disappeared into the wilderness with no trace. Search and rescue was called, and countless hours were logged hoping to find these lost souls. Of course I assumed they found some, but Craig Dale's book "The Daunting" was not about the lucky ones - it focused on those not so lucky.

Craig Dale's book was very detailed in the exact times and locations of those that disappeared, and I could only imagine the footwork he had to do in finding his facts for this book. I quit reading the circumstances and just read the names of those that had gone missing for the next several chapters. None of the names as I read them out loud jarred a memory of who they were. Each page of names added to my astonishment of how many folk had disappeared in Rocky Mountain National Park - I had no idea.

Just reading the names now quickly and not the circumstances and swiftly moving the pages with the tip of the eraser of the pencil, I then came to a chapter entitled *"The Modern Mountain Men."* The beginning of the chapter reads, *"Of course, all those mentioned before this chapter may not be all that surprising given the nature of those that had disappeared. The common thread was they were young or very old. Even those in good physical shape and should have known better seemed mentally and physically unprepared for the remote mountains and the thin air associated with the higher altitudes. None were skilled in the way of the mountains and the adverse weather that can occur in the remote regions of Rocky Mountain National Park."*

This chapter will concentrate on the men that were more than capable of handling this high frontier. They were men that were born out of time with the instinct for wilderness survival of those from a forgotten past. They were men trained for these mountains and high altitude conditions - not to conquer them, but to embrace the dangers of the high country. Some had fought in the jungles of Vietnam while others had climbed the highest mountains not only in Colorado but those of the rest of the world. These men mentioned in this chapter were men among men. They in earlier times would have been the gladiators and kings. They all to a man were physically fit, strong, intelligent and more than capable of surviving the harsh and remote environment of Rocky Mountain National Park, yet they still marched into the wilderness to never again be heard from. They, like all the others not prepared, also disappeared."

Craig Dale quickly cut to the chase and listed *"The Modern Mountain Men"* that had vanished into the thin air in Rocky Mountain National Park. The first name was Micah Trask my long-lost friend.

"Micah Trask - 27-year-old Colorado native who lived in Granby, Colorado which is situated in Grand County, Colorado vanished in Rocky Mountain National Park on Saturday 9/16/1972. Trask served two tours overseas as a Special Forces Weapons Sergeant in the most famous of the Special Forces involved in the Vietnam War - the United States Green Berets. Trask was assigned to the 5th Special Forces Group out of Nha Tran. Micah Trask was also a mountain climber who with his best friend Dane Lee were well on their way to conquering the 58 mountain peaks that were 14,000 feet or higher commonly known as the 14ers in Colorado. As of 1972 they had climbed 39 of the 58 mountains, including two of the most difficult ones being Pyramid Peak of the Elk Mountains near Glenwood Springs, Colorado and the formidable Longs Peak which happens to be in Rocky Mountain National Park - the same park that Micah Trask disappeared in several years later. Micah Trask was experienced in the way of the mountains, yet he also vanished into thin air."

More than a few tears formed in my eyes as I read the short description of my best friend. It was factual but did not touch on the person I knew as Micah. His heart was genuine, and his love for animals surpassed his love of mankind. He had been my best friend, and I missed him so. Not a day goes by I do not think of him and all that we had done and accomplished together in our friendship. After Micah disappeared, I never attempted to climb anymore of the 14ers. At first I was waiting on him to come home so we could finish the task. After a couple of months had passed, I realized he was not coming back and I lost interest in doing so. It was supposed to be Micah and me against the high mountains together. It just didn't work out that way. Wiping the tears from my eyes, I continued to read.

"Kevin Kyriss - 31 years old and like Trask was a veteran of the Vietnam war after serving three tours and begin awarded two silver stars in service there. Kyriss lived and worked as a hunting guide in the area and surrounding mountains of Walden, Colorado. He was born on a high mountain ranch and was known as a mountain man to the locals of Walden. An accomplished man, yet during an autumn hiking and fishing trip, he also disappeared in the wilderness of the Rocky Mountain National Park on Saturday 10/21/1972 a little more than a month after Trask vanished."

"Shawn Lord - 43 years old lived in Vail, Colorado. Shawn had accomplished what Trask and his best friend were trying to accomplish. He had conquered all the 58 14ers in Colorado and almost lost his life in a failed attempt to reach the summit of Mount Everest in the Himalayas. Lord vanished into the unknown in the Rocky Mountain National Park on Saturday 10/13/1973. He had been staying in Grand Lake, Colorado and using the park as a training ground for what he hoped was a successful second attempt on Mount Everest. It was not meant to be since he was swallowed up into the wilderness as well."

Having reached the end of the page, I once again used the eraser of the pencil to move the page off of the stack to continue reading. My heart dropped for what I saw on the next page. The page was empty and white as snow. I quickly looked at the remaining pages and they also were blank. It would seem I had seen and read all that Craig Dale could tell me - this was how far as he had gotten in his book titled "The Daunting."

CHAPTER 13

My mind was going here and there trying to make sense of all that I had read in Craig Dale's book or for that matter what I had not read. I tried to piece together what I had learned and what I already had known.

What I already had known was about my best friend Micah and when and where he disappeared. Assuming that Craig Dale was correct in his investigation, what I had just learned from the manuscript "The Daunting" was the brief summary of who Shawn Lord and Kevin Kyriss were as people and that they like Micah had disappeared in Rocky Mountain National Park. The summary of Kevin Kyriss' case was he vanished roughly a month later than Micah, and Shawn Lord faded into the Rocky Mountain mist about a year later than Micah. The only connection among Micah, Kevin, and Shawn were that they were all, just like in Craig Dale's book, modern mountain men - men who knew how to survive in the harsh environment of the high altitude. They were tough men that were situated in the fast changing environment of Rocky Mountain National Park, but had vanished in the park nevertheless.

Sitting at Craig Dale's desk reminded me that Mr. Dale had also gone missing and if what I thought was true, he also had vanished in Rocky Mountain National Park. Looking about the room, I once again focused on the fantastic nature photography of Mr. Dale, but there were three other photos across the room I barely glanced at before. Someone hung them next to each other in a horizontal line. Standing up, I slowly crossed the room to look at the photos. As I got closer, I could see they each were framed 8 x 10 photos of a lone man standing on top of a mountain peak in the summer snow still evident on the granite peaks and big white cottony clouds in the background. Each photo had a caption underneath the man and reading left to right:

Craig Dale
Mount Elbert - 14,439'
Craig Dale
Torreys Peak - 14,275'
Craig Dale
Quandary Peak - 14,265'

These photos were not taken by Craig the photographer; these photos were of Craig as he stood at the top of the world. It would seem that Craig Dale was not only one of the best nature photographers I had ever seen and a budding author writing his first book, but also a mountain climber conquering the over 14 thousand foot mountains of Colorado. Craig Dale was a modern mountain man himself.

Looking at my watch, I was surprised that it was already ten minutes past noon. It seemed the morning had slipped away from me as I headed down the stairs to the first level. After I opened the front door, the now freezing wind hit me, prompting me to once again pull up the collar of my coat to cover my ears. Stepping out and taking Micah's key, I locked the door behind me. Looking at the whiskey half barrel planter that Micah had used to conceal the key so many years ago, I decided not to hide the key again and took the time to slip it onto my keyring.

After planting my butt in the seat of the Grand County Sheriff's Blazer, I waited a few minutes, letting the engine warm up since the temperature had dropped since this morning. Snow had started to gently fall from the sky with about two inches of accumulation on the blacktop of the highway. Grabbing the police radio mic without dropping it, I pressed the transmit button and said, "Dispatch, this is Dane Lee. I am done with my initial investigation at Craig Dale Photography and back on the road. Have I missed anything exciting?"

The police radio crackled twice with a second of silence in between before Yvonne the dispatcher replied, "Nothing exciting Dane. Gene is out on the pump road just south of Grand Lake at the Roy and Baldwin spread. It would seem someone shot one of their cows sometime during the last twenty-four hours. Nickey and an ambulance are in route to a single vehicle rollover one mile west of Fraser."

Thinking about what dispatch had said, I opted out of the cow shooting since it was not a rare occurrence especially during hunting season. More than likely an accident from a stray bullet that traveled further than intended by the shooter not taking care of being aware of the background of what they were shooting at and probably did not even know they had shot the cow. Shifting the manual transmission into second, I headed eastbound on Highway 40 in the direction of Nickey Lynn and the one vehicle rollover.

After getting into the correct lane of travel, I pushed on the gas pedal slightly to gauge the slickness of the road, and the rear end skidded back and forth some indicating below the fresh snow was a blanket of black ice. Pulling over onto the shoulder of the road, I got out and manually rotated the front locking hubs into the 4x4 mode. Getting back in, I once again pulled back onto the highway with the confidence of better traction having all four wheels grabbing the road.

Grabbing the police microphone again and once again not dropping it, I pressed the transmit button. "Officer Chavez, in route to your rollover to see if you need assistance."

The radio crackled several times until finally the voice of the woman I loved came over the airwaves. "Copy that Undersheriff Lee. A Ford pickup did a 180 roll and now is resting on its top with minor injuries to two occupants. Be advised that the road is icy under the snow. Pickup slid on the ice and then rolled into the bar ditch on the north side of the road trying not to hit a raccoon that darted in front of them. Could use some assistance in traffic control until One Eye Zach and his tow truck get here."

The snow was getting thicker, and the wind was increasing for a possible October blizzard. Keying the mic once again, "Copy that Officer Chavez on the ice. Be there shortly."

Reaching down, I turned the radio on to my favorite country station and the man in black Johnny Cash. I was just about to the end of his song that explained why he always wore the color black. The song was released several years ago, but I liked it as well today as the first time I ever heard it. I mean really who does not like a Johnny Cash song? *"Believin' that the Lord was on their side..."*

Driving more slowly than normal due to road conditions gave me time to go over again what I had learned from Craig Dale's book "The Daunting." It was an unknown factor how Micah, Kevin, and Shawn - accomplished and wilderness savvy men - could simply disappear in an environment they knew so well.

Craig Dale fit the same profile of those known to have disappeared, yet it was unknown whether he had disappeared in Rocky Mountain National Park as well.

There were four other names that were on that list as well that I knew nothing about at this moment in time. It had now become my mission to learn more about Samael Amos, Bryan Amen Jerry Toney, and Randy Weems.

Bryan Amen, who had been Gene Sanford's sister's old boyfriend according to Gene, also fit the profile of a modern mountain man. Hopefully Gene's sister could shed light on Bryan and what he is up to now. My gut instinct and my belief was that Bryan had also gone missing as the others, but I needed Gene's sister to either bolster this claim or disprove it. My hope was Bryan was alive and doing well, but I feared the worst.

When I get back to the office at the end of my shift, I would have to detail in a report to the sheriff everything I had learned so far from Craig Dale's home and business with no assumptions on my part. Sheriff Walker was not a man that liked assumptions - he wanted facts - cold hard facts. I had more assumptions than facts, so it would be a short report I handed the sheriff tomorrow.

After climbing Red Dirt Hill, I passed the historic YMCA of the Rockies Snow Mountain Ranch and then quickly traveled through Tabernash as Highway 40 now took more of a southern shift onto the flats of Fraser Valley. The snow had started to let up enough I could see the red and blue flashing lights of Nickey's Grand County patrol Blazer a couple of miles down the road.

Once reaching the accident, I sat in my sheriff's Blazer surveying the scene, and I noticed One Eye Zach the tow truck driver from Granby was already on site and had already righted the Ford F-250 pickup on to its wheels and was hooking up the winch cable to pull the truck out of the ditch. By the looks of it, the pickup would be a total loss. A middle-aged man and woman were being treated by the ambulance crew and seemed to have escaped the rollover with minor injuries which was a welcome sight. Nickey in her usual efficiency had roadside flares out and was standing out in the cold and slightly gusting wind waiting to direct traffic, but there was not one vehicle as far as I could see in both directions on the highway.

Nickey of course had noticed me and making sure she was looking my way, I rolled my window down and made a big show of rubbing my hands together and then placing them on the top of the dash as if I was getting the warmth from the heat that flowed from the window defroster. I continued to stay in the Blazer acting as if it was too cold outside and I was just fine where I was all nice and warm. Nickey Lynn saw my dog and pony show and did exactly what I expected her to do - she flipped me the bird. We both smiled and laughed and just as I was about to go join her in directing the non-existent traffic, my police radio crackled and Gene Sanford came over the air, "Officer Sanford to Undersheriff Lee!"

Since I was already half out the door of the Blazer, I made an awkward grab for the transmit mike and it sprang out of my hand like a black coiled snake and ended up on the passenger side floorboard again. I hate that shit! Squaring my butt back into the seat, I waved at Nickey and then closed the door. She placed her hands on her hips in disbelief and then flipped me the bird again. Smiling, I was able to retrieve the police radio mic by fishing it toward me by pulling on the black coiled mic cord. Once I had the transmit mic under my control again, I replied to Gene, "Go ahead Officer Sanford, this is Undersheriff Lee. Are you still at the Roy and Baldwin spread?"

There was silence for almost a full minute before Gene replied, "Negative Dane. Not much to report on the cow shooting and writing the report back at the office. I just got off the phone with my sister. Earlier I called and told her about Bryan's name being on the list and that you would like to speak with him. She called his mom in Denver and you will never guess what Bryan's mom told my sister!"

Without missing a beat, I keyed the transmit button and replied, "That Bryan Amen has gone missing in Rocky Mountain National Park!"

Total silence for a full minute before the radio crackled again, "Wow! That is affirmative Dane! How did you know?"

CHAPTER 14

I rolled it around some in my thinker before I answered. I confirmed all roads in this unknown scenario led to Rocky Mountain National Park. Bryan Amen, Kevin Kyriss, Shawn Lord, and of course Micah Trask had now, according to what we had found out had over the last four years, disappeared in the high mountains of "The Park." Craig Dale was missing, but not confirmed yet from where; if my gut instinct was correct, we will find out soon enough that he just like the others disappeared in The Park. Samael Amos, Jerry Toney, and Randy Weems were the lone leftovers from Craig Dale's list.

Still rolling all that I had learned around in my brainpan, I watched Nickey Lynn as she chatted with the driver of a 1972 Chevy Pickup as he stopped to survey the tow truck as it struggled to pull the wrecked F-250 from the bar ditch.

Pushing the transmit button on the mic, "Following a hunch Officer Sanford, my gut told me that is what we would find out about Bryan Amen. If you are finished with your report from the Roy and Baldwin cow shooting, I need you to track down what type of vehicle Craig Dale drives. Once you have that information, call up the ranger station at Rocky Mountain National Park and see if they have any abandoned vehicles they are keeping an eye on within the boundaries of the park."

The police radio hissed once before Gene replied, "Roger that Dane, doing it as we speak."

Pulling my collar up to cover my ears, I opened the driver's side door of the Blazer and stepped out into the cold wind and made my way to where Nickey was standing all by herself now that the Chevy pickup driver's curiosity was satisfied about the wreck and what happened.

The ambulance left the scene without lights flashing with the older couple who had just rolled their pickup to the small non-emergency clinic in Granby. Zach was finally able to get the totaled Ford F-250 winched out of the ditch and loaded on to his flatbed for hauling to Granby to his yard for storage until the owners and or the insurance company decided what they wanted to do with the wreckage.

Nickey and I both waved at One-Eye as he sped up as he passed us heading toward Granby leaving Nickey and me all alone on the now deserted highway between Fraser and Granby.

Nickey turned to me with that smile I loved so well and she stood on her tiptoes and kissed me full on the mouth which of course I reciprocated. I loved this woman more than life itself - there was no doubt about that. It was as if I was walking in a mist until I met her and she cleared the sky and brought the sun and the warmth into my life. There was nothing I would not do for Nickey Lynn Chavez.

The snow had stopped completely, and the sun poked its warming rays out from behind the fast fading gray storm clouds as Nickey and I stood on the empty highway basking in the new warmth of the sun and the old warmth of each other.

Taking a few minutes, I brought Nickey up to speed on what I had learned so far today. I told her of reading and scanning Craig Dale's unfinished book and the possible fate of Kevin Kyriss and Shawn Lord according to what Mr. Dale had written. I also spoke of what Gene Sanford had found out about Bryan Amen from his sister and that he, like Micah and the others, had vanished in Rocky Mountain National Park.

After hearing me recite what I knew for the facts, she searched my face to see if I had any more information and deciding I did not she finally replied, "Wow Dane, all of this going on with the disappearances in Rocky Mountain National Park and no one had a clue or at least tied them all together except Craig Dale. What do you think is the next step to take?"

Nickey had asked the obvious question, and I took several seconds before answering. "My gut tells me that Samael Amos, Randy Weems, and Jerry Toney have gone missing in Rocky Mountain National Park as well and we need to concentrate on that to see if that is true. We already know Craig Dale is missing. We just don't know from where just yet. I have Gene trying to find out what type of vehicle Mr. Dale drove and the park rangers' office in the park is trying to see if they have any abandoned vehicles that possibly could be Mr. Dale's. What my gut is not telling me Mi Vida is why they have all disappeared. All the clues so far have added up to "The Park" being where they were, but nothing so far points to the why."

What I didn't mention to my lady love was that in my mind, I was already convinced those that had gone missing had been murdered because in the dreams with my grandfather, I saw a buck knife sticking out of Micah's chest. Having a knife poked into your chest was not an accident, but something sinister. The words from the dream that grandfather had spoken kept coming back to me as well. *"Dane the tasks before you are simple enough and you already have the path to follow, for it leads to the mountains and the wilderness. Follow the sign and the tracks. Find out where your enemy is. Get after him as soon as you can. Strike him as hard as you can. Have no remorse, for he is evil, then move on."*

The sun had already melted the snow, and there was a thin layer of black ice on the highway pavement as was the way in the high country of Colorado during the early autumn months. The snow had cleansed the air and when I filled my lungs with each breath, it felt invigorating and gave me strength, but not the knowledge I was seeking. I needed some place where I could think clearly without distractions. Looking at the woman who had stolen my heart, I said, "Find out from dispatch if there are any more pressing matters that need to be addressed and if not head to the sheriff's office and find out what you can about Samael Amos, Randy Weems, and Jerry Toney. I am going out to the horse property to check in on Cochise and Thunder."

A smile crossed over Mi Vida's face as she said, "My man needs his horses to clear his mind and to gather his thoughts, which I understand perfectly."

Nickey Lynn knew me better than anyone else, and she understood my best thinking was when I was with the horses. Reaching up and gently touching her cheek with my right hand, "As you know I ponder the best out there with only the horses around; it must be the Ute Indian in me."

Nickey reached up and touched my cheek lovingly and with her eyes showing she was in deep thought, she said, "I feel a storm brewing within the mountains and that a great battle is near and that we will be in the center of it!"

Somehow this woman had reached inside me and peeked at my soul, for I felt the same that something was out there and it would be a battle to the death with no glory - just death. Micah's disappearance, along with the others and the dreams of my grandfather, was building to some sort of climax, of what I did not know currently. Trying not to alarm Nickey, I said, "I did not realize Mi Vida that you had Indian blood in you as well!"

A smile slowly crossed Nickey's face as she turned to head to her Blazer. Just as she opened the door, she looked over her shoulder back at me and said, "Not Indian blood, Mister. I have hot Catholic, Mexican blood from my dad and sensible East coast, Jewish blood from mother's side running through my veins!"

There was a reason that I thanked the Lord above every day for having this woman share my life with me. She was a rock – a hot Catholic Mexican with a sizable portion of East coast, Jewish type of rock!

As I watched Nickey pull onto the highway, pointing the hood of her Blazer towards Granby in the distance, I heard the police radio crack and hiss before hearing Nickey. "Dispatch, this is Officer Chavez and leaving the scene of the rollover near Fraser. Is there anything else that needs my attention?"

Yvonne spent no time replying, "Negative Officer Chavez. The phones have been quiet since the Roy and Baldwin cow shooting and your rollover."

Nickey replied, "Copy that dispatch, I am in route to your position."

Pulling on to the quick drying pavement, I headed back toward Granby. Reaching down, I turned on the radio and since I was heading to the horse barn to spend time with Cochise and Thunder, it seemed only fitting that a song released about a year ago by Michael Martin Murphey named Wildfire was playing. *"Oh, they say she died one winter…"*

I spent about an hour with Nickey's three year old gelding Appaloosa Cochise and my Mustang mare Thunder grooming their tails and manes with a wooden curry comb. They both were loving the extra attention on this day, and it made me realize once again next to Nickey how both of these horses were the most important aspects of my life. I have always been drawn to horses, and they have always been a big part of the Ute Indian culture. It is one thing to own horses, but another thing altogether to be one with them. Most folks didn't understand that last part, but in my family horses were a way of life. My dad used to say, "All a man needs for happiness was a good horse, a good gun, and a good woman. All in that order." Nickey and my mother would argue the order of that happiness, but not the sentiment.

After much thought and pondering, I had no new insight to the disappearance of my best friend Micah and the others, but feeling fresh and renewed after spending some alone time with the horses, I loaded up myself in the county Blazer to head back to the office.

Once on the road the police radio crackled and Gene spoke, "Undersheriff Lee, this is Officer Sanford."

Pulling over, I spied the radio microphone and with slow determination, I was able to grab it without dropping it and was proud of myself for doing so. Smiling to myself, I pressed the transmit button, "This is Lee. Go ahead Officer Sanford."

Without hesitation and with just a small hiss of lost airtime Gene answered, "According to county records Craig Dale has a registered 1974 Toyota Land Cruiser the color red with Colorado tags MTNMN 709. I just got off the phone with a park ranger named Sam, and he told me they have a matching Toyota with that license plate they have been keeping an eye on for several weeks waiting for the owner to come back from what they hoped was a prolonged hiking trip."

Well, I guess that confirmed what my gut was telling me that Craig Dale the nature photographer and author had gone missing like the others in Rocky Mountain National Park.

CHAPTER 15

Once I got back to the sheriff's office as per my routine, I stopped in front of the missing poster of my long lost best friend. Reaching up, I touched the face of Micah Trask as I always do and closed my eyes for a few seconds with my finger still pressing the aging photo. This time touching the photo differed from what it had been the norm in the last four years. This time I felt as if maybe, just maybe I was on the right path to find out what happened to my friend. Slowly taking my fingers off the photo, I spoke with a whisper, "I have never forgotten, my friend. I feel a reckoning on the horizon!"

The rest of the afternoon went by quickly even though there were no more calls such as accidents or citizens of Grand County needing help. Gene and Nickey Lynn were working the phones and county records within this office trying to track down any information that was readily accessible regarding the remaining names on Craig Dale's list - Samael Amos, Randy Weems, and Jerry Toney.

I worked on the report I would give to Sheriff Walker tomorrow on the now reported missing Craig Dale to bring him up to speed on what was happening and where this new investigation was heading and adding that the park rangers in Rocky Mountain National Park had located Craig Dale's 1974 Toyota Land Cruiser within the park's boundaries, which would require further investigation. As I was typing the report, I realized in all reality, I didn't have much in the way of facts. Just a lot of speculation on my part in reading the not completed information taken from an unfinished and unpublished book.

From the beginning of the day until now, I documented everything I knew at this point and from re-reading it twice, I knew in the mind of the sheriff it would sound shallow and with a ton of speculation on my part. Thinking it was best, I added in the final paragraph of the report that we were in the process of trying to corroborate Craig Dale's claims of those modern mountain men that had gone missing in the park. Micah Trask was a no brainer since we did in fact know he had gone missing four years ago in the park.

After pulling the freshly typed letter through the rollers of the typewriter, I blew on the ink trying to help it dry faster to prevent any smudges. Nickey approached me with an outstanding idea and said when she had the time tomorrow she would head over to the Grand County library in Granby and use their microfilm reader and look at all past newspapers they had on microfilm to match up the names Samael Amos, Randy Weems, and Jerry Toney. She would also try to match the dates following Weems's and Toney's names to any newspaper articles.

After laying my report on the investigation of Craig Dale gone missing on Sheriff Walker's desk, I got Mr. Dale's sister Patty Dale's phone number from the memo that Yvonne had filled out when she placed a call to Belle Fourche, South Dakota to inform her we concluded that her brother was indeed missing and that we would look into the matter further. I assured the obviously concerned Miss Dale that we would do anything within our power to find the answers she was looking for. I also added that she should inform us immediately if Craig should contact her in the meantime. My gut instinct told me that Mr. Dale would not be making any phone calls now or in the future. It was phone calls such as these that made being a law enforcement officer difficult and heartbreaking.

After our shift Nickey left for home fifteen minutes before I did and she said she would start dinner. Stopping once again on the way out to look at Micah's missing poster, I had a sense of urgency come over me. I felt the answers to his disappearance were coming fast and hard - maybe too fast.

In the autumn and early winter, darkness comes early in the Rocky Mountains, and the sun as I stepped out the door of the sheriff's office was already starting its arc below the mountains in the western horizon. Stopping for several minutes, I watched the sun and the brilliant orange and dark blue, cloudless sky slowly disappear and become one with the night. Later, once all traces of the day were gone, the stars would own the heavens and rain down their twinkling light on all that I love. The weather here in the Rocky Mountains could be harsh and deadly, but despite this it also brought grandeur and beauty to the high country. I have lived all my life in the same country as my ancestors. I have never felt cheated on not seeing the rest of the world; I felt privileged to live here. Smiling, I thought to myself, "That must be the Ute Indian blood in me."

As I shifted into second gear and slowly let off on the clutch, my Grand County Blazer and I pulled out onto the blacktop of the highway and headed home. When I turned on the radio, Willie Nelson was singing a tune I knew - not my favorite Willie song, but a song called "Uncloudy Day" which proved once again that my life had a soundtrack. *"Oh, they tell me of a home far beyond the skies..."*

The roads were clear and dry and nearly vacant for my commute home and after several Waylon and Willie songs and in less than fifteen minutes, I was home.

Nickey already had the dinner of Mexican rice with pork green chili and fresh tortillas ready, and I promised her tomorrow night it was my turn to make dinner. We both laughed because Nickey Lynn has been just as unimpressed with my culinary skills as she was with my coffee making skills, and we both knew there was no way in hell she would let me loose in her kitchen. So after every meal, I promised to make the next one knowing full well she would decline my offer. It had now become a running joke between the two of us and never ceased to bring a smile on Mi Vida's face.

We set up coffee trays in the living room so we could watch Monday Night Football with Howard Cosell the wordsmith and the former Detroit Lions player Alex Karras. This game featured the two best all-around coaches in the National Football League, Pittsburgh's Chuck Noll and Minnesota's Bud Grant. It was a game of defense and at the end of the game, Minnesota would win 17 to 6.

After the football game and washing the dishes together, Nickey and I hardly spoke. It was not until we went to bed that we spoke in very eloquent terms, and hardly a word was uttered as we made love.

After we both were sweat drenched and satisfied, Mi Vida kissed me one last time before rolling onto her side as sleep overtook her.

Still trying to catch my breath, I thought about what just happened in our love making; it was different tonight and more hot, heavy, and physical and more like the first time we ever made love. It was great, but different. I pondered why that was. Nickey's and my intimacy had always been more than physical; tonight was even more so in the sense it was almost as if we could reach into each other's soul and find out they mirrored one another. Tonight it was all about her and it was all about me at the same time like no one else in the world mattered, and it felt good to be selfish in the sex and of course the intimacy. Reaching over, I touched Nickey's back and could feel her heartbeat as she breathed in and out. Tasting the salt of my sweat once again, I could only think of one thing - if I had not already known it until tonight, it was driven home that Nickey Lynn Chavez and I were soul mates. When we were apart even for short periods of time, there was always something missing and when together we felt that everything was perfect in the world and the stars were aligned just the way they should be.

Then it came to me in a flash why tonight of all nights was different. It was as if I felt something threatening and unknown was just out of reach in the darkness. Hell, I think we both felt it and that was the reason to be more urgent and resolved in our lovemaking almost like it would be the…last time! Once that thought crossed my mind, the feeling of dread that had been building all day as we gathered increasingly more information about the disappearances in Rocky Mountain National Park, finally built to a crescendo. Looking at the love of my life as she slept, I got scared.

CHAPTER 16

Finding sleep was difficult because my brain pan was on overload trying to make sense of all that I had learned so far today. The feeling of trepidation was building to an unknown conclusion, and it worried me that somehow not only did it involve Micah, but also Nickey Lynn as well - it was a disturbing feeling I could not shake.

After several hours of watching Nickey enviously as she peacefully slept without a care in the world, I finally fell asleep and it was not long when the dream with grandfather returned.

This time the dream was still in the autumn months as the dream before, but now there was snow on the ground about twelve inches deep and the air was chilled with ice crystals as they floated in the air. Once again, I was walking down the same wilderness trail that felt more than familiar, and it baffled me why I could not recall the name or location, because my gut instinct told me I had walked this trail many times before. The crow from the previous dream was still sitting on the same evergreen limb as before, and its ebony black feathers seemed almost to have a shine to them as they shimmered in the low light of a cold, late autumn day. The crow and the message it represented spoke to my Ute Indian blood as no other spirit animal could. The crow I knew was a warning of a life mystery and death, which even though I was dressed for the weather, gave me a sudden chill throughout my body. The crow once again twisted and looked to the ground, and the snow at the base of the tree started to ooze crimson - blood red. A lot of blood, more than one person's body could ever hold, but that of many people. Death was under the snow and all around me in this place. It was a killing place - this wilderness trail was where Micah and possibly the others had died - I knew that now. Micah's body was not here in this dream, nor were any of the others that had vanished, but I knew this was the last place they had been alive. Feeling a new presence behind me, I slowly turned and there was grandfather as before, sitting on a rock ten feet away whittling a piece of aspen wood with a large Bowie knife. Grandfather's apparition was my height and weight and he looked like me - just older with shoulder length hair white as snow. Grandfather stopped his whittling and looked directly into my soul for what seemed an eternity before he spoke with a commanding and deep voice the same words as before, "Dane the tasks before you are simple enough and you already have the path to follow, for it leads to the mountains and the wilderness. Follow the sign and the tracks. Find out where your enemy is. Get after him as soon as you can. Strike him as hard as you can. Have no remorse, for he is evil, then move on." Not knowing how to answer, I said nothing and then I noticed a shadow of a man lurking and standing still a short distance behind grandfather. I focused on the shadow trying to bring out any detail I could make out of the outline of the shadow man. My gut instinct was triggered again, for I knew this man - this shadow man - was the one I was seeking - he was the evil that grandfather spoke of. He was the one that had taken the life of my best friend. Suddenly the man in the shadows raised his arm as if he was reaching out to touch me.

Startled and bathed in sweat, I could feel the touch of someone's hand on my chest. I flipped my eyes open and grabbed the wrist of the hand touching me. Nickey Lynn was just as startled when I grabbed her wrist violently. It took several seconds to realize it was the woman I loved who had placed her hand on my chest. Releasing her wrist quickly I said, "I am so sorry Nickey. I was having a bad dream!"

Nickey pulled back slightly from leaning over me as she gingerly massaged her wrist where I had grabbed her and she spoke out not in anger, but concern. "No shit Sherlock, I have been trying to wake you for several minutes."

Raising my eyebrows slightly before replying, "No shit, Sherlock?"

Nickey's eyes and concern lifted and then evaporated as her smile slowly spread across her face, and we both chuckled as she faded into my arms and I hugged her as if there was no tomorrow. Holding Mi Vida tightly, I didn't want to let go. That sense of anxiety and dread I had been feeling did not leave when I woke up from my dream. It was going to be a long, long day.

Five o'clock came quickly as both Nickey and I got ready for work. It was my morning to take care of Cochise and Thunder, so after a quick breakfast, dressing, and belting on my 357 Ruger Blackhawk, I left. Nickey's plan was if there was nothing pressing, after checking into the sheriff's office, she would head to the Grand County library and the microfilm reader to see if they had any old newspapers mentioning the remaining names on Craig Dale's list - Samael Amos, Randy Weems, and Jerry Toney.

The horses were happy to see me this morning and after spending an hour with them grooming and feeding them, I left and they seemed content to let me go about my day. The sun was just peeking above the mountains to the east as the night stars lost their luster and faded into the ever reaching blue sky for the day. The wind was absent and silent this morning, and the temperature was actually very pleasant for the start of a typical Rocky Mountain autumn day.

As I pulled out on the road and pointed the hood of the county Blazer toward Hot Sulphur Springs and the office on this crisp autumn morning, I turned on the radio and the one-year-old Waylon Jennings' song came over the airwaves that was a tribute to the one and only Hank Williams Senior – "Are You Sure Hank Done It This Way." "*Lord it's the same old tune, fiddle and guitar…*"

Singing along with Waylon, I thought about him and his hold over my musical taste. First off, his cassette tape – Waylon's Greatest Hits - was Micah's and my go to tape for traveling music. Whenever we traveled around the state climbing the 14er's,

Waylon's tunes were what we listened to. Waylon was originally a bass player for Buddy Holly. After Buddy's death, Waylon followed with his own act and became one of the founding members of the "Outlaw Movement" of country music that included such greats as Willie Nelson, Johnny Paycheck, Kris Kristofferson, Johnny Cash, Merle Haggard, David Allen Coe, and George Jones. Jennings was also married to the exquisite Jessi Colter, who is the "First Woman of Outlaw Music." Of course I loved Waylon and his very distinctive voice and passion for his music, but his hold on my taste had more to do with the man himself. He was a rebel and an outlaw that went against the grain in country music. No rhinestones for Waylon and the other outlaws. He was a man among country singers. Loved that about him, and I also loved the outlaw image he portrayed. I saw myself like that when things went astray, thinking I would handle any difficult situation in my way and go against what was considered normal. The Ute Indian blood that flowed in my veins gave me a different outlook on life in general, and my sense of justice was more aligned with that of my ancestors of old. That last thought about justice made me chuckle some and then my thoughts ran the gauntlet. "Dane Lee, thinking like that might not be a good thing!"

After reaching the office, I paused in front of Micah's missing poster as always and touched the aging photo. It was a ritual I was hoping to break once I found out the "why" and "how" of why my friend vanished into the wilderness.

After planting my butt into the chair at my desk, I saw there was a note from Nickey, saying she would be at the library doing her research on those men that had gone missing and still not accounted for. As I sifted through last night's reports on the happenings in Grand County, my mind drifted and I wanted to go be with Nickey Lynn at the Grand County library, but knew I would only be in her way since I did not understand how the microfilm reader worked. Nickey said it was simple really and explained that a microfilm reader is a device used in projecting and magnifying images stored in microform to readable proportions. Microform includes flat film - microfilm in this case - where old Grand County newspapers were hopefully stored on open reels. They often use microfilm to store many documents in a small space. Hell, it sounded complicated. Nickey was more up on the new technology of the day than I was and was more equipped to do this part of the investigation.

As I was trying with some difficulty to finish my paperwork, Sheriff Walker came to work. He grabbed his first cup of coffee for the day and headed to his office to read the reports that were on his desk including mine on the disappearance of Craig Dale. About thirty minutes passed, and I heard the voice of my boss as he shouted through his open door into the squad room, "Dane Lee, get your butt in here!"

CHAPTER 17

As I stood in the doorway of Sheriff Walker's office, he let me wait as he read my report on Craig Dale once again as he was seated at his desk. He then looked over the top of his glasses at me and finally said, "Take a seat Dane."

Sitting down, I could tell that Tom was perturbed, but not angry. He took off his glasses and laid my report down on his desk and leaned forward with his elbows on his desk and then he spoke, "It would seem that Craig Dale as of yesterday has officially been reported as missing from what I read in your report. And from the memo from Yvonne about the phone call from Craig Dale's sister in South Dakota, it would also confirm that. And it would seem that you have also put in time searching the office and home of Craig Dale Wilderness Photography. Am I correct in adding that all this sheriff's office has so far is from Mr. Dale's unpublished book called 'The Daunting?' It would also seem that this book being written by Craig Dale is also unfinished and unpublished. That to this date we have no corroborating evidence to back up Mr. Dale's claims these men have all gone missing in Rocky Mountain National Park. Am I assuming correctly?"

I knew my report was slim and after I heard the sheriff's summary of my report, it seemed even slimmer than slim. I scratched my throat as I coughed to clear the saliva that had formed as well before I spoke. "Yes, sheriff that is all we have so far. Officer Chavez is over at the Grand County library trying to track down old newspaper accounts to corroborate what Mr. Dale has written. It would also seem that Mr. Dale's Toyota Land Cruiser has been abandoned in Rocky Mountain National Park for several weeks and the rangers have been keeping an eye on it to see if the owner was just on a prolonged backpacking and hiking trip. The rangers now know as of yesterday we have reported that Craig Dale, the owner of the Land Cruiser, is officially missing."

Sheriff Walker took his elbows off the desk and clasped them behind his head as he leaned back in his chair as he thought it over what I had just said. He took several minutes before he spoke. "This is damn interesting for sure Dane, even if it is all circumstantial for now. I will give the green light for Officer Chavez, Officer Sanford, and you to follow up on any and all leads you come across not only in Dale's disappearance, but also the others as well including Micah's. Mind you, no overtime on this - just regular hours. Now get your butt out of my office and get to work."

Standing up swiftly, I turned to leave and Sheriff Walker spoke again. "By the way Dane, nice work."

Back at my desk, I pulled out of the top drawer a photo of Micah and me at the summit of Pyramid Peak in the Elk Mountains. Touching the photo, I said out loud, "Getting close my friend, getting close."

After a full minute looking at the photo and reliving that climb in my memory, I pinned it to my bulletin board just below the note of the missing men from the book "The Daunting." Just as I had finished that small task, Nickey Lynn came storming in and laid several copies of articles of some old Grand County newspapers and a copy of the actual newspaper on my desk and sat down hard in the chair in front of my desk. She obviously was excited as she pointed at the copied newspapers on top of the not copied newspaper, saying, "I have circled the news stories you need to read."

I picked up the first copied one and looked at the top of the page at the date which was 9/10/1973, a Monday. There was no photo to match the article, and the article was short and to the point. *"Randy Weems age 32 from Kremmling, Colorado. Officials reported the former Army Ranger and local hunting guide missing in Rocky Mountain National Park while rock climbing last Saturday 9/8/1973. They called the ground and air search and rescue operation looking for the whereabouts of Mr. Weems this morning at eight after an overnight snowstorm dropped eighteen inches of snow in the area of the search."* It would seem that Randy Weems not only went missing in the park as the others, but from what was briefly written he also fit the profile of the men who like Micah were modern mountain men.

Setting down the copied newspaper clip, I looked at Nickey Lynn as she smiled at me caught up in the enthusiasm of the investigation. Nickey pointed at the next article and said, "There is more Dane, keep reading."

Picking up the next copied article, I once again looked at the date 10/11/1974 a Thursday and just a tad more than a year after Randy Weems had vanished into the thin air of Rocky Mountain National Park – *"Jerry Toney a world famous mountain climber from Alzada, Montana who had previously climbed the highest mountain in the world Mount Everest at 29,029 feet above sea level in Nepal had been staying in Grand Lake, Colorado for several weeks as he trained for an attempt of climbing Nanga Parbat the ninth highest mountain in the world at 26,660 feet above sea level which is located in the Diamer District of Pakistan's Gilgit Baltistan region. Nanga Parbat is the western anchor of the Himalayas. Historians derive the name Nanga Parbat from the Sanskrit words nagna and parvata which together mean 'Naked Mountain.' Nanga Parbat is also a notoriously difficult climb. Countless mountaineering deaths in the mid and early 20th century lent it the nickname 'Killer Mountain.' Park officials reported Jerry missing in Rocky Mountain National Park in Colorado on Saturday 10/5/1974. The ground and air search and rescue operation was called off this morning as a snowstorm blanketed the area that was expected to drop two feet of snow. With no new clues to the whereabouts of Jerry Toney, officials decided it did not want to put searchers in harm's way."* After I read this copied news story, it jarred my memory, and I remembered it because it had reminded me so much of Micah. At the time I dismissed it in my mind as Jerry Toney had simply fallen in his training, and his body would be located sometime the following spring by some hiker. Obviously he also fit the profile of the modern mountain man and it would seem to date they have never found his body. Nickey, while I was reading, had gotten up to get us both a cup of coffee and put the steaming mug down in front of me and then pointed at the newspaper saying, "The article you need to read is at the top of page twelve."

Picking up the newspaper, I looked at the date 10/1/1976, last Friday. Dropping the page down, I looked at Nickey before speaking, "Did you pick up the wrong newspaper by mistake Nickey? This is from last Friday."

Nickey's eyes got wider as she replied, "No mistake Dane, just go to the top of page twelve and read."

Somewhat confused, I did as she asked and picked up the paper again and turned to the top of page twelve. There was a black and white grainy photo of a park ranger standing in front of the Rocky Mountain National Park sign which was located on the other side of the Continental Divide at the Estes Park entrance. There was a caption under the photo which read *"Supervisor Park Ranger Samael Amos at the Estes Park entrance of Rocky Mountain National Park."* Speaking out loud and not to anyone in particular, "What the hell?"

Nickey scooted up to the edge of her chair and as she got closer she said, "Keep reading Dane."

The article was short and to the point – *"Samael Amos a Rocky Mountain National Park Ranger will add this year when the park opens a new guided trail hike on the Chapin Creek Trailhead. Ranger Amos will begin his guided tour from the Chapin Creek Trailhead, located roughly 6.7 miles from the point where Old Fall River Road becomes a one-way dirt road. Originally opened in 1920, Old Fall River Road was the first route to cross the Continental Divide in Rocky Mountain National Park. Traveling only eleven miles now, the road extends from Horseshoe Park to Fall River Pass. Please dress accordingly."* Thinking hard, I looked at Nickey Lynn and said, "It would seem that Samael Amos is alive and well and a park ranger to boot. What are your thoughts, Officer Chavez?"

Getting caught up in the moment of the mystery of the disappearances, Nickey smiled before she spoke. "Obviously the reason there was never a date after Samael Amos' name on Craig Dale's list is because he never went missing. I thought about this on the way back to the office, and it made sense that Ranger Amos was Craig Dale's source for information for his book 'The Daunting' and the disappearances of the others. Before I left the library, I called the park to speak with Mr. Amos and it would seem that he was off today. After explaining to the ranger office that I was an officer in the Grand County Sheriff's office, I then asked for his phone number, and the person I spoke with said Samael did not believe in phones and didn't have one, but he provided his address in Grand Lake which he said was a small cabin at 1220 3rd Street."

After I listened to Nickey's thoughts, it sounded reasonable that Amos had been or would be interviewed by Craig Dale for his book. Picking up the newspaper again, I studied the grainy photo of Samael Amos and even in the poor photo, you could tell that Amos was about my age with dark hair and judging him by the sign behind him, he was maybe a tad taller and heavier than I was. You could see his biceps bulging underneath his short sleeve ranger uniform. In this photo he looked to be in tremendous physical shape, but that would not be surprising given the nature of his job. Feeling better that the investigation into Craig Dale's disappearance was still going forward and had yet to stall, I smiled at Nickey before I spoke. "It would seem Nickey my love that the next step would be to interview Samael Amos."

Nickey quickly stood and asked with a smile, "Do you want me to handle it, Undersheriff Lee?"

Standing up myself, I said, "I think I will follow you over Officer Chavez since this is the only lead we got so far."

Just as I had said that, Sheriff Walker appeared at my desk and handed me a telephone memo from the park rangers in Rocky Mountain National Park asking what the sheriff's office wanted to do about Craig Dale's red Toyota Land Cruiser since the owner had been officially reported missing. The sheriff quickly added his two cents to the subject and then quickly turned around and left, leaving no room for debate. He had said, "Dane I need you to run up to the park and check this out ASAP. The park rangers want to know if they need to mount their search and rescue operations."

Thinking that would be the next step and was glad that the sheriff had brought it to my attention, I turned to Nickey and said, "I will go to the park and check out the Land Cruiser. Why don't you have Gene follow you over to Grand Lake to get him out of the office since all he is doing is reading a copy of Mad magazine."

Nickey looked in Gene's direction, and he was indeed reading his latest subscription to Mad with the usual cartoon caricature of Alfred E. Neuman, the fictitious mascot, on the cover. Nickey's eyes smiled as she looked at Gene and then back at me and then once again at Gene before she spoke. "Officer Sanford, I know you are busy, but would you like to go to Grand Lake to talk to a real park ranger?"

Gene laid down his copy of Mad magazine and his eyes got large, chuckling before he replied, "You mean like a Smokey the Bear type ranger?"

Nickey and I both laughed at that before Nickey with a half chuckle replied, "Yes, just like Smokey the Bear. So saddle up Officer Sanford because daylight is burning."

Gene jumped to his feet and threw his Mad Magazine on his desk before saying with a childlike demeanor, "Cool!"

CHAPTER 18

Nickey Lynn, Gene and I, when we walked by Micah's missing poster, touched it as we walked out of the door. It was as if all of us had come together as one and were acting as a single person in the quest to find the answers to Craig Dale's disappearance and the others including my long lost best friend Micah. As we all got into our respective Grand County Sheriff's Blazers, I felt renewed in the sense that at least the sheriff's department and I seemed to be moving in the right direction in finding out what happened to Micah over four years ago.

The day matched my mood as there were zero clouds in the forever blue above my head. The sun was shining, and the wind had taken a vacation for now. The aspen trees dotting the mountainside were less golden color as autumn was making its final push toward the fast closing winter months. It would not be long and all the aspen leaves would be gone for the year. The Rocky Mountain seasons – as life – were a constant, never-ending cycle of rebirth and death. It was the same as it was when my Ute Indian ancestors and my famous Grandfather Matt Lee walked these mountains of old. This everlasting cycle of life and death spoke to the Indian side of me.

Nickey pulled out first, then Gene, and then myself as we headed eastward on Highway 40. Feeling good about the day, I popped a John Denver cassette into the player, and it was already fast forwarded to one of my favorite songs of his that reminded me of Micah, "Rocky Mountain High." *"His sight has turned inside himself to try to understand..."*

Following the Colorado River as it zigged and zagged along the highway, we made the west side of Granby and the Highway 34 junction in short order. We headed northbound toward Grand Lake which was where Nickey and Gene were heading to interview the park ranger Samael Amos and where I would continue on even further north into Rocky Mountain National Park to check on Craig Dale's Toyota Land Cruiser and speak to the park rangers there.

Passing Lake Granby on the east side of the road, I noticed that some ice had built up on the edges since the last time I had driven by here. There were several hardy fishermen along its shores enjoying the day. More fisherman were dotted along the shore of Shadow Mountain Lake as well. I thought that if Nickey and I had not been working, it would be a great day to fish.

Just past the general store and gas station on the highway was the road. We veered off east from Highway 34 that would become the West Portal Road and the main drag of Grand Lake Village that Nickey and Gene took as they now were heading into town. Passing that exit, I continued on north to Rocky Mountain National Park. Reaching down and grabbing the police radio microphone and pleased with myself for not dropping it, I depressed the send button and said, "Officer Chavez, make sure you take notes and see if Mr. Amos has any copies of anything he might have given Craig Dale in his research for his book."

There was a moment of silence before the radio crackled and Nickey responded, "Copy that, Undersheriff Lee."

Continuing north several miles, I came to the entrance of Rocky Mountain National Park that had several rangers working the booths and gates letting folks in once they paid or showed their yearly pass. Trail Ridge Road, the highest paved road in the world, would close in the next couple of weeks when the snow at those lofty heights would become unmanageable for the road crews. Trail Ridge always closed about the third week in October and would not reopen until the end of May the following year.

There were several cars at the crossing gates paying the fee and getting information for their day travels from the rangers as I pulled over to the side of the road. Cranking down my window halfway so I did not lock myself out, I left my county Blazer and the heater going to keep it warm when I stepped out into the crisp Rocky Mountain autumn air. I did not envy those that lived in Denver in what some locals here called the "Big Smoke" due to the ever present brown cloud that hovered over the city. I could not imagine having to breathe that smog of pollution that choked the city down there at the bottom of the foothills. Life here was cleaner and simpler. Just the way I liked it.

There were two rangers working the booths, and I knew both. Brett Hooper was in the class behind me in high school and we were friends and had gone fishing together several times although not in recent times. He was about six feet tall with blonde hair, a friendly sort with always a smile on his face. Sandee Adams was from Denver originally and was a very attractive petite blonde that had been a park ranger for over five years. I had dated Sandee casually up until I met Nickey Lynn, but we were still on friendly terms and knew each other well or about as well as those that had been intimate with each other.

All the cars that had been waiting to enter the park had paid their dues and had left, leaving the road abandoned for now. Since Sandee and Brett had a few minutes in between the tourists, they stepped out to greet me, Brett with a hardy handshake and Sandee with a small kiss on my cheek. Sandee spoke up first with a smile, "Well Dane, you are looking as handsome as ever and with the uniform and your six shooter, you must be here in an official capacity today. How is your lady doing?"

Sandee never called Nickey by name - it was always "your lady." Smiling, I said, "Nickey Lynn is doing fine and I will tell her you asked about her. As for the visit it is official; I came here to look at an abandoned Toyota Land Cruiser and a missing person case."

Brett spoke up in his official capacity as a park ranger and said, "The red one; we heard someone from your office would be here today. I will call ahead and get one of the rangers working the roads to come down and lead you to it. We had been keeping an eye on it and as one week turned into two weeks, we feared the worst."

Brett went back to his booth to make the call and left Sandee and me standing outside in the high mountain air when I asked her a question. "Do you know the park ranger Samael Amos?"

Sandee's smile evaporated, and she seemed to be in some deep thought before she replied, "Of course I do; he is one of our supervisors. Samael is like you Dane in some ways, and then not like you in other ways. He is very handsome and muscular and built like you, but taller. He spends all of his free time here in the park even during the winter months. He is a mountain climber and likes to explore the most remote areas of the park. He knows this park better than any man alive - that is for sure. He does his exploring all alone, and he told me once he was born 150-years too late and that he would have been the greatest mountain man of all time. Between you and me, he is an arrogant SOB. He looks at me and the others as we are just pieces of meat and we are beneath him because we do not take fitness as seriously as he does and that he thinks he is smarter than the rest of us. Other than that Dane, he is a nice enough fellow."

The last sentence was said with a chuckle, and it reminded me that Sandee was not only beautiful, but one hell of a woman. If I had not met Nickey, then I would probably still be with Sandee. Just as I was about to reply, five more cars showed up to enter the park, and Sandee smiled and said as she hurried to her booth, "Hold that thought, Dane."

Stepping quickly aside so the cars could pass, I wandered over and leaned against my Blazer as I waited for one of the field rangers to come down and show me where Craig Dale's red Toyota Land Cruiser was. I thought about what Sandee had said about Samael Amos, and I gathered he was not a likeable fellow by any means. And it seems he was a loner to boot. Thinking back to the first time I had read his name on the top of Craig Dale's list, I remembered what Nickey Lynn had told me about the name Samael. *That it was one of the Jewish myths, Samael was the grim reaper and a fallen angel. He is known as a destroyer and a seducer. He is also known by names like the Prince of Darkness and the chief of the Dragons of Evil.*

Just as that thought ran its course through my mind, the police radio crackled and hissed until Nickey Lynn's voice came over the radio loud and clear, "OFFICER DOWN - ALL UNITS - OFFICER DOWN - NEED ASSISTANCE AND AMBULANCE ASAP 1220 3RD STREET, GRAND LAKE."

My mind went numb for a second as the radio went dead, and before my mind caught up to my body and I could move, the radio hissed and crackled again with the woman I loved in a voice that was losing its strength, "DANE - HURRY!"

CHAPTER 19

Once my mind caught up with what I had heard, I quickly got in my county Blazer and with one look back at Sandee who had a puzzled look on her face, I shifted into gear and did a U-turn back on the highway as I turned on my lights and siren and headed back to Grand Lake - Nickey was in trouble.

As I reached down to grab the police radio microphone, it sprang out of my hand and landed on the passenger floorboard. In trying to retrieve it, I veered to the right and almost drove off into the ditch on the west side of the road. After regaining control of the Blazer, I thought to myself, "Calm down Dane, you are only a few miles away. Won't do anyone any good crashing into the ditch before you get there!"

Taking a calmer grab for the elusive microphone, I was able to pull the black coiled cord until I had it in my right hand and before I could transmit, Sheriff Tom Walker came across the radio, "All available units proceed to Grand Lake - address 1220 3rd street. Officer down - ambulance in route. Use extreme caution; we do not know any particulars yet! Dane Lee, what is your twenty?"

My heart was beating furiously in my chest as I pushed the transmit button, "Sheriff I am just ten minutes out! Nickey Lynn, if you can hear me, I am on my way!"

Working my way through town, I turned off my lights and siren and once I turned south on Jericho Road, several cars and trucks passed me heading north over the arched bridge and canal that connected the waters of Grand Lake and Shadow Mountain Lake. Turning east onto Main Street, I could see Grand Lake at the end of the road and Bald Mountain hovering over the water in the distance in the east. After stopping, I pulled my 357 3-screw Ruger Blackhawk and added one shell that I always kept in the chamber empty under the hammer for safety. Not knowing what was ahead of me, I slowly drove down the gravel road on Main Street east until I came to the curve that turned south and became 3rd Street just on the edge of the water of Grand Lake.

Once on 3rd Street I could see both Gene's and Nickey Lynn's county Blazers parked nicely on the west side of the road. Nickey's Blazer was in front of Gene's and had the passenger door open. Whatever happened occurred after they got out of their vehicles since there was no panic or alarm when they simply had parked.

Stopping a half block away, I turned off the ignition and slowly and cautiously stepped out onto the gravel of 3rd Street with my 357 Ruger drawn and ready and made my way forward until I could finally see the small cabin that was at 1220 3rd Street. The cabin was typical for Grand Lake and made of lodgepole pine that grew abundantly on the surrounding mountains. What was not typical was that Gene Sanford's body, drenched in blood – a lot of blood - was lying on the small front porch. From this distance Officer Sanford's body seemed stiff and lifeless, but where was Nickey?

Noticing the front door of the cabin was wide open as if someone had just left for a minute to check their mail, I moved forward. Knowing Nickey had made a transmission on her police radio, I moved from the driver's side of Gene's Blazer across the back to the passenger side. Having done that, I saw Nickey was lying on her back on the ground next to her opened passenger door in a puddle of crimson.

Moving quickly to her side with my weapon at the ready, I saw no movement other than Nickey was struggling to breathe.

Bending down, I could hear the sirens of the cavalry on its way. The face of the woman I loved was bleeding profusely from what looked like a crisp, clean knife cut. I knew she was close to death and in a bad way. As I moved closer to a position where I could hear her, Nickey's eyes snapped open and with a faint voice and with blood forming in air bubbles on her lips she said, "Dane, that bastard Amos killed Gene by slicing his throat and then he turned on me before I had a chance to draw my gun! He gave us no warning or indication; he attacked before we even said anything like a cornered animal once we stepped up to the porch! Then he disappeared, and I heard a vehicle leaving. I did not get the make or model!"

With a tear in my eye, I bent down and grabbed Nickey's hand as I looked in her eyes as they clouded over and said in a calmer voice than I was feeling, "Hang on Mi Vida, I got you now. Hang on Nickey; you have to fight!"

Reaching into her Blazer, I located her trauma kit that was standard equipment for all Grand County Sheriff's department vehicles. As Nickey had gone silent, I took my knife and cut her sheriff issued uniform blouse and quickly opened it to survey the damage. What I saw made my heart drop and do a double flutter as there were three distinct puncture wounds, and her lifeblood was flowing out of her body. How she had survived this long before bleeding out was a miracle. Knowing she only had a few minutes if that before she died, I had to try to stop her bleeding.

Remembering my training that dealt with bullet wounds, I saw no difference in these puncture wounds made by a knife, and I knew a sucking chest wound or wounds can lead to a collapsed lung. Locating the blood stopper compression bandages, I applied them as I had been taught during police training, knowing full well that for now this was the only way to stop the sucking and bleeding by closing the open wound. I tried to be as quick as I could, but gentle as well knowing Nickey's spine could also have been damaged in the knife attack or could be damaged more by any attempt by me to save her life. Nickey had gone unresponsive after telling me that Amos was the attacker, and I feared the worse. If her heart, lungs, spine, or a large blood vessel were damaged, there's not much I could do outside of getting immediate expert medical care. The paramedics would be here shortly, but expert medical care that Nickey would need was in Denver 2 ½ hours away. If anyone ever needed the Flight for Life helicopters from St. Anthony Hospital out of Denver, it was Nickey Lynn Chavez.

As the sirens were getting closer and having done all I could do to stop the bleeding, I stood up and reached into Nickey's Blazer and keyed her police radio transmitter. "Be advised one officer is dead and another is critical - advise Saint Anthony in Denver we need their Flight for Life."

Yvonne the dispatch immediately answered, "Calling Saint Anthony Denver now!"

Once I knew the helicopter was being dispatched, I keyed the transmitter once again, "Murder and assault suspect is named Samael Amos and should be considered armed and dangerous. Amos is a Rocky Mountain National Park employee and has left the scene in an unknown vehicle!"

Thinking about that, I probably passed him on the way here as he was fleeing. The only way out in a truck or car from 3rd Street was over the arched bridge and then through the town of Grand Lake back to Highway 34.

Kneeling down, I felt for a pulse in Nickey's throat, and she was still very much alive. The compression bandages seemed to have stopped the bleeding for now, and I hoped and prayed for the woman I loved. Grabbing her hand, I stroked her palm with my thumb and spoke to her not knowing if she could hear me. "Nickey my love, this is not your day to die! I need you more than ever. You are what completes me and everything I will ever do in my life I want to share it with you. I got a helicopter coming and they are going to fly you to Denver to fix you all up. You can't die on me yet - I will not allow it!"

Nickey's eyelids fluttered, and they opened barely, but they opened and she tilted her head to look at me and in the faintest voice whispered, "I am not going to die, Dane; you have not learned to make a decent cup of coffee yet. My job here and with you is not finished."

As several Grand County Sheriff's Blazers and an ambulance come to a sliding halt, Nickey Lynn tried to smile, but her face was not having it. My tears started to flow after hearing her speak, and the guilt hit me like a sledgehammer. I had let her down and she could die from my poor judgment. If only I had sent her to the park instead to check on Craig Dale's abandoned Land Cruiser and I had come here to interview Samael Amos. Choking back my regret, I told her my thoughts. "I am so sorry Mi Vida that I was not here to protect you!"

Nickey Lynn was still struggling to keep her eyelids open and her breathing was shallow as she fought to live, but her eyes found mine and the cloud lifted for a second as she faintly spoke to me, "Not your fault, Dane. You are here now and that's what counts." Grasping my hand tighter she spoke again, "If I die Dane, you have to avenge me! Promise me that!"

The woman I loved knew she was on the verge of death, and there was nothing I would not do to save her life. And if the Lord saw fit she should die, there was nothing I would not promise her. "You fight Nickey! You fight hard! As God is my witness, I will avenge you Nickey Lynn!"

CHAPTER 20

Sheriff Tom Walker and every available Grand County Sheriff Deputy had responded, most of which were out of uniform since it was their day off. There were even two highway patrol cars I could see within the sea of red and blue flashing lights. The paramedics spent little time with Nickey Lynn before loading her on a gurney and into the ambulance since I had already contained the bleeding. Nickey was now unresponsive as I held her hand as they loaded her up, and then one of the paramedics pushed me backwards and told me flat out there was not enough room for me in the ambulance and that I would only be in the way as they worked on Nickey. For a split second I was angry at the man that was trying to save Nickey Lynn's life, but quickly realizing he was correct, I stepped back as they closed the back doors. With numb and teary eyes, I could see through the two small square windows, and the paramedics had gotten an oxygen mask on Nickey and were working feverishly trying to stabilize her as the ambulance pulled away with its lights flashing and the siren blaring.

Standing there watching Nickey and the ambulance fade into the evergreen trees as they rushed her away, I felt all alone in the world. There were more people than I could count here at the cabin, but Nickey Lynn Chavez was my life, and I realized even in my confused state of mind that this may be the last time I would ever see Mi Vida alive again. I felt utterly alone.

Sheriff Walker joined me and said, "I have notified every police agency in the state, and they now are looking for Samael Amos as we speak. They quickly are putting up roadblocks at all the main highways in or out of Grand County. All that can be done is being put into motion."

Looking at my boss, I almost felt dead on the inside as once again the guilt of putting Nickey Lynn and Gene Sanford in harm's way took hold of my body and soul. Looking past the sheriff, I could see a police crime investigator taking photos of Gene's body already as he lay bloodless and cold on the front porch of the small cabin. Trying to clear my mind, I asked Sheriff Walker, "Is Flight for Life on its way?"

Sheriff Walker grabbed my shoulder with a fatherly touch and said, "Yes, they have dispatched it and will meet the ambulance somewhere on the highway so they can move Nickey into the helicopter. Trust me son, everything that can be done to save Nickey's life is being done."

I looked at the sheriff but actually looked past him as my mind focused on Samael Amos. Talking to myself, but out loud so the sheriff could hear me, "He went to the park; it is the only place he will feel safe."

Sheriff Walker looked at me for a few seconds and his face showed not only concern, but also confusion before he spoke, "What did you say, Dane?"

Shaking my head to clear the last image of Nickey being carted away in the ambulance, I said, "Samael Amos is a man of the wilderness, so he will head to the only place he feels safe and that will be somewhere remote in Rocky Mountain National Park! When he left here, he was only ten minutes away from what I am sure he felt was his sanctuary in the park. The big question is, why did he attack Nickey and Gene?"

The sheriff shook his head in understanding and said, "We have men inside the cabin as you can see looking into the why." If that is the case Dane, and he has headed to Rocky Mountain National Park, he would have already been inside the park before any roadblocks could have been set. He would have had to drive by the entry gates and we will know for sure he is there. It is my feeling if he is hiding there, we will get him before nightfall. That park is unforgiving. We will shortly have a special weapons and tactical team out of Denver, and we will start canvassing the park. He can't go far."

Sheriff Walker was a seasoned professional and had been involved in more than a few manhunts in his service in Grand County, but my gut was telling me this man Samael Amos was a different breed altogether. I think time will show my gut to be proven right. Without knowing why, I had a sense of the man being someone born out of time and that Rocky Mountain National Park was not only his backyard, but also his home and where he felt alive. He will have the ability to fade into the remote wilderness. My thoughts, I am sure, to Sheriff Tom Walker were a stretch and for now I will keep them to myself. The only thing I thought was a proper response for now was, "I hope you are right, Tom!"

I stepped up and onto the front porch as the sheriff moved away to talk to the highway patrol officers present as they were all working on the logistics of the manhunt trying to corner the suspect Samael Amos with roadblocks. At first I looked at Gene. His face looked almost peaceful in death and besides his throat cut open and his life source congealing on and around his body, he looked as if he could just be asleep. Hard to believe just an hour before he was reading his "Mad" magazine and thinking it was "cool" to meet a real life park ranger. One of the crime techs named Kellie Hooper was standing guard over Gene's body and the entrance to the cabin. She thought about stopping me from entering the cabin, but quickly changed her mind when she saw the determination on my face and my uniform now caked with Nickey Lynn's blood.

Standing there at the doorway were two crime techs going about their jobs in an efficient and professional manner as they photographed the interior of the cabin. From my vantage point, it was obvious that Samael Amos was a man to be reckoned with. This cabin of his was more like a war room of sorts. I could see several weapons that were out in plain sight such as an Italian Beretta Model 92 handgun and a Heckler and Koch HK MP5SD which was the suppressed version of the classic HK MP5 submachine gun made in Germany. Both guns were some of the latest weapons of warfare, and I wondered how Amos could get hold of them. I had only seen photos of both in magazines and never one up close. Not your typical weapons you would see in Colorado or along the Rocky Mountain frontier in 1976.

As I looked about, it was also clear to me that Samael's cabin was just a place to sleep, his way of staying normal in the modern world. In the few minutes I had been standing at his door, I remembered what Samael had told Sandee Adams about his being born 150 years too late. His cabin had zero comfort in the way of the modern world. No television, no radio, no electric or gas fired cook stove. There was not one single electric lamp or overhead light. Just a wooden-framed bed and a wood fire cook stove, which was as far as I could see his only warmth for the high mountain winters. Since the cabin was only a one room affair, I also could tell there was no bathroom with running water. Stepping back out the door, I saw beyond the considerable amount of stacked wood what I thought at first glance to be an abandoned outhouse forty feet to the west. Obviously it was not abandoned and still in use. This was Samael Amos' world outside of Rocky Mountain National Park. This cabin was not home in the normal sense of the word - it was a lair - such as a wolf, bobcat, or fox would use. It was a lair of a very dangerous animal named Samael Amos.

There were several faded Polaroid snapshots thumbtacked to the wall next to the front door, and I had to squint my eyes in the low light of the cabin to focus on them. Each and every photo was of Samael. No friends or family - just Samael Amos. Knowing I would never know the answer, I wondered who took the photos.

Until now the only photo I had seen was the one in the newspaper this morning that Nickey Lynn had dug up. It was black and white, grainy, and out of focus and it was difficult to see Samael's face in it. These Polaroids here on the wall, although faded and yellow with age, were much better and in color, so I could finally get a good look at the man himself.

The one Polaroid that caught my eye the most was a full body shot of Amos standing in an aspen tree grove, and by the color of the leaves it was in the beginning of autumn. Just like Sandee Adams had said, he looked and resembled me in many ways. He was obviously in tremendous shape and seemed to be a tad taller than I was. We had other similarities aside from the physical and that he was armed in the photo with a holster and what seemed to be a 357 3-screw Ruger Blackhawk just like the one I had on my hip right now. He had foreign weapons here in his lair, but it seemed his preferences in firearms were the ones made here in the good ole' USA. Just like me, he was a Ruger man.

It was in 1955 when Ruger introduced the Blackhawk chambered for the 357 Magnum cartridge. The Blackhawk replicated the size of the old Colt Single Action in both frame size and grip size. The Blackhawk also had adjustable sights mounted on a flattop frame like many of the custom Colts and Colt Single Action target models. Besides replacing the Colt flat springs with coil springs for better durability and using a frame-mounted firing pin, the lock work of the Ruger Blackhawk was very similar to that of the Colt. The Blackhawk hammer had four distinct clicks that could be heard while it was thumbed back to full cock, which was characteristic of the Colts. The cylinder was free spinning, but for loading the hammer had to be placed at half-cock, another characteristic of Colts and older single action revolvers. Because the lock work was so similar to that of the Colt, the Ruger Blackhawk had three screws on the side of the frame just as the Colts did. This model 3-screw Blackhawk is commonly referred to as the "flat top" due to its flat top strap.

In his right hand above his holstered 357, Samael Amos was holding a Ruger Mini-14 rifle. The Mini-14 was first introduced in 1973 and was a lightweight 223 caliber semi-automatic rifle with a self-cleaning, fixed-piston gas system. The Mini-14 was a short rifle at three feet and one inch and light, weighting only 6 ½ pounds. The Ruger Mini-14 had a rear aperture sight with large protective wings and no integral scope bases.

To complete what a modern mountain man might wear, Amos also had a black handled Buck knife in a sheath on his left side. Once again just like me. Probably the same one he used to cut Officer Sanford's throat and to stab Nickey.

Wanting to have the photo of the man that may have in time killed the woman I loved so I knew what he looked like, I unpinned the Polaroid from the wall and placed it in my rear pocket with none of the crime scene techs noticing me. Feeling guilty for taking the photo from a crime scene, I jumped when the crime scene tech said, "Undersheriff Lee, you might be interested in this."

Turning around, I saw the tech pointing at the wall just to the right and above of the wooden-framed bed. As I stepped closer after the tech had shot several photos, I bent down to look at what he had pointed at and had just photographed. It would seem that Samael Amos was just like most modern mountain men; he collected trophies. Thumbtacked to the wall just like the Polaroids were six different drivers' licenses lined up with one on top of the other. From the top to the bottom the names read - Craig Dale, Bryan Amen, Jerry Toney, Randy Weems, Shawn Lord, Kevin Kyriss, and my best friend Micah Trask.

CHAPTER 21

Seeing Craig Dale's license at the top drove home the assumption that Mr. Dale was dead. I already knew that, and I did not need another dream and chat with my Grandfather Matt Lee to confirm it. Legally until someone found a body, he would always be presumed missing. I knew better. As I continued to study the thumbtacked drivers' licenses of those that were missing, it would seem that Samael Amos was not only a man who was very dangerous and not to be taken lightly, but also a serial killer.

Sheriff Walker came to the front door and said, "Dane, could you step outside. I need to talk to you."

Hearing those words from the man I respected almost brought tears to my eyes. Thinking the worst and fearing that Nickey Lynn had died, I reluctantly followed the sheriff out. Once outside I waited a few seconds for Tom to begin to speak. Clearing his throat and with a worrisome look Tom said, "Nickey is still alive, and they have transferred her to the helicopter and they are flying her to Saint Anthony's. The doctors and surgeon have been made aware of her grave condition and are preparing for her arrival. The good news is - if there is any good news in all of this - the paramedics said what you did for Nickey before they got here probably saved her life."

Nickey was still alive! My knees buckled, and I almost went down, but the sheriff reached out and helped me keep my feet and my dignity. Feeling small and trivial in the world at this moment, I looked at Tom and he spoke again, "Samael Amos did in fact flee to Rocky Mountain National Park as you suspected. He drove around the gate without stopping and his 1975 Ford F-250 was found just now abandoned on the road and he is now on foot. The highway patrol has his truck under observation, and they are waiting for the arrival of the special weapons and tactical unit from Denver. The way I see it any man who would panic and ran like Amos will be captured or will be dead before tomorrow morning. And before you say anything Dane, you are not going to the park. I feel it would not be wise for you to be there since this man attacked Nickey. I cannot have you going off half-cocked and shooting this guy when he is captured. This one has to be done by the numbers. Having said that, I have Yvonne booking you a hotel room near Saint Anthony's at county expense, and you as of this moment are on paid leave of absence. You need to be there for Nickey. Go home and pack for an extended stay. I will be in touch every day with updates."

My initial reaction was anger at the sheriff for putting me on paid leave. Then I rolled it around some in my thinker, and I knew my old friend was correct in doing what he had done. He was doing his job and making the right decisions even if in my sorrow I did not think so. My gut instinct was telling me that Samael Amos did not panic and being on foot was probably the cleverest thing for him to do. My thought was that Amos would have been shrewd enough to know eventually he would be found out and he would have planned for it. He would have set up a hidey hole somewhere in the remote part of the park. It was exactly the same thing I would have done in his position. He didn't panic at all - he went home to roost in his new lair. Although I hoped the SWAT unit would capture Amos, I had my doubts. Samael Amos was now in his environment. He was a modern mountain man with the skills of the old mountain men. I knew in my heart it was meant to be that I would be the one to confront Amos. It was my destiny, and I could feel it in my bones and the Ute Indian blood rushing in my veins. But for now I would do as my boss and my friend had asked because it was the right thing to do. I had to go to Nickey - she needed me in the worst way. Having decided to do as the sheriff had asked, I reached out to shake his hand and said in a calm and effortless voice, "I understand Tom, and you are right and for now I need to be at Nickey's bedside, and I appreciate you and the county for the opportunity to do that."

Sheriff Tom Walker with a manhunt to conduct dismissed me in his mind and left me to my own thoughts. Climbing into my Grand County Blazer, I sat down hard into the driver's seat. It was at that moment, after seeing all of Nickey's dried blood now caked on my uniform, the magnitude of the situation was brought to bear on my mind and soul. As I started the engine, I cried as my emotional roller coaster took a big dip with not a few tears, but a full out flood of tears. As I crossed the arched bridge over the connecting canal between Grand Lake and Shadow Mountain, I could hardly see the road or the reporters now converging on the scene of Gene's death and Nickey's attack.

As I turned south onto Highway 34 to head to Granby, there seemed to be a never ending sea of law enforcement vehicles that included the highway patrol and the neighboring counties' vehicles flowing north into Grand Lake and Rocky Mountain National Park. All men and women that had a man to catch and a job to do - my job. My mind was cluttered with rampant emotions of love, hate, and of course, guilt as I blindly and without thinking and out of habit reached down and turned on the radio and the Willie Nelson song from his Red Headed Stranger album was just starting. "Blue Eyes Crying in the Rain" which was probably the saddest song ever written and recorded. *"When we kissed goodbye and parted..."*

As I listened to the whole song, it made me realize that what had happened today and with Nickey's life hanging in the balance, my life just like a moving picture show had always had a soundtrack if I knew it or not. I turned off the radio because the music that had always brought happiness to my life and Nickey's life brought only sadness and memories. If she died, that music...that happiness... would be no more. Until this retribution for the man that killed my friends Micah and Gene and who had attacked Nickey, had occurred, I could no longer listen to that soundtrack that played behind in the background of my life.

Before I got to Granby, I checked in with Yvonne back at the office, and she informed me that Nickey had made it to the hospital and was being prepped for surgery. Yvonne told me she was praying for her which I appreciated the sentiment.

I needed to check on Cochise and Thunder before I left, and I also needed to arrange for their care while Nickey and I were down in Denver. Our neighbors also boarded their horses on the same property, so that should not be a problem getting them to care for Cochise and Thunder for an extended time. We had done the same for them when one of their folks had gotten sick and passed away.

After cleaning up and washing off Nickey's blood, I packed some of my belongings and a few things for Nickey. The 2 ½ hour trip to Denver seemed to take forever as I drove with my mind in a fog. Once I was up and over Berthoud Pass, my police radio became silent since I was no longer in range. I turned on the Blazer's radio to the news station KOA out of Denver, and the manhunt for Samael Amos in Rocky Mountain National Park had become national news, and they were giving updates every half hour. Each report started by mentioning that one Grand County Deputy had been killed and one critically wounded without revealing Gene's or Nickey's name. Not one mention of finding the drivers' licenses of the missing men - Micah, Craig, and the others. It was still early in the investigation and I am sure Sheriff Walker did not want to broadcast that Samael Amos was a possible serial killer.

The night had come on suddenly and with the darkness as I went over the top of Floyd Hill on Interstate 70, I could see the city lights sprawled out before me, flickering and sparkling at the base of the Rocky Mountain foothills. Just as I passed the exit to the town of Morrison, another update came over the radio. And the last words of the news reporter after giving his update echoed what I feared the most. *"It would seem that Samael Amos, who was a known radical survivalist with extraordinary wilderness skills, has faded into the remote mountains and has vanished."*

CHAPTER 22

Saint Anthony was located just off of West Colfax, and Yvonne had gotten me a room in a mom and pop motel not more than three blocks away. After checking into the motel and getting the key, I never even looked at the room and headed directly over to the hospital. Nickey was out of surgery and was in intensive care and once I found her room, I looked upon her as she lay sleeping under heavy medication with all the IV tubes and the oxygen mask. Her color was ashen, and I feared the worst as she fought to live. They had stitched the cut on her face and it looked angry and swollen, but she was not struggling to breathe, and that was a huge step in the right direction.

After several hours of my prodding the nurses to talk to the surgeon that had worked saving Nickey's life, he finally came to her room to give me an update. He was hesitant to talk to me since we were not married and her folks had yet to arrive from Arizona, but he finally sat down with me as I held Nickey's hand. He explained all the medical jargon which I had a hard time following, but the final analysis was that she was very lucky that first off I was able to control the bleeding when I first found her and secondly that the good news was that no major organ had been damaged. She was not out of the woods yet, but with time and some extensive therapy, he thought she could have a full recovery. I almost kissed the surgeon when he stated that.

I tried to sleep some of the night in a chair in Nickey's room as a parade of nurses were in and out and to my untrained eye, Mi Vida seemed to get the best of care. One of the female nurses mentioned that reporters from the two local newspapers "The Rocky Mountain News" and "The Denver Post" as were reporters from the local news television stations were camped out in the waiting room hoping to get the latest on Nickey's condition.

I stepped out several times to stretch my legs but avoided the waiting room and the reporters; there was no way in hell I wanted to talk to them. On these trips out of Nickey's room, I could catch some news coverage at the nurses' station of the ongoing manhunt. There were several news stations on hand and were filming from a distance. I could see numerous SWAT members and law enforcement personnel moving anxiously about on the ground and several helicopters were visible with searchlights as they flew above the tree lines and over the mountains. Sheriff Walker was interviewed, but I could not hear his words since the nurses kept the volume off as not to disturb the patients in ICU, but the strain and worry on his face spoke to me. By all accounts Samael Amos had disappeared. My gut instinct told me he was holed up in his lair waiting out the search.

Later I fell asleep and the recurring dream of grandfather and the remote and lonely wilderness trail began again. It was the same dream on the same wilderness path that kept nagging at me with frustration since I should know where it was, but didn't. At the end of the dream grandfather gave me once again the same message as before. *"Dane the tasks before you are simple enough and you already have the path to follow, for it leads to the mountains and the wilderness. Follow the sign and the tracks. Find out where your enemy is. Get after him as soon as you can. Strike him as hard as you can. Have no remorse, for he is evil, then move on."*

Bolting awake, I was bathed in a cold sweat and my first response was to look at Nickey. She was still under medication and sleeping about as peacefully as she could considering her grave condition. I thought about the dream, most of which had come true so far. At this moment of time I even knew who my enemy was and that he had vanished into the mountains and the wilderness of

Rocky Mountain National Park. The wilderness path in the dream I felt was the key; somehow it was tied to Amos' hidey hole and lair. I tried to rack my brain to gather more details from my dream about this trail or pathway and I was getting nothing - nothing at all. One thing I felt certain was the manhunt for Samael Amos would turn up empty. He was too good in the wilderness, and my gut was telling me he had planned his escape well in advance. My Ute blood and mountain man instinct told me to end this ordeal with Amos; it was for me to do and me alone. I couldn't care less why Amos did what he did; it only mattered to me that he attacked and almost killed Nickey and that he had killed Micah, Gene and the others. There was to be a reckoning in the future. I just did not know when.

Considering my training in wilderness survival, I knew I was an equal match to Samael Amos in the skills of the mountains and the high country. Knowing Amos was a cold-blooded killer, I knew the difference would come down to if I had a "killer instinct" or not. On more than one occasion I had spoken to my dad and his dad about this and the history of the Lee clan going all the way back to Grandfather Matt Lee, also known as the "Ghost." Now looking back on it, I think I was being prepared by the spirits of my ancestors the Ute people and my mountain man bloodline for this showdown with Amos. Concentrating on those long ago talks about having a "killer instinct," I recalled what my dad had said. "Remember Dane, you must have the ability to put your mind outside your body and focus on the only thing that matters at that exact moment of time before you draw your pistol or knife. You must have the ability to place your fear of death aside. You need to have a black heart, and you have to be able to focus on all things that could affect the outcome, such as the placement of the sun, the wind, or even a droplet of sweat. All this focus has to happen in the mere seconds before, during and after you have decided to take your enemy's life and draw a weapon. You have to become a killer in all sense of the word and go against everything you had ever read in the bible or have been taught by modern society. The bible taught us we are supposed to forgive those that have harmed us or the ones we loved. As much as we want to believe this to be true, you have to realize that man has and will always will be a predator. As in the way of the mountains, wilderness, and nature, only the strong survive. In the wild in the Rocky Mountains the bear, mountain lion, and the wolves are king, because they are stronger and more cunning than the rest. It is the same for man; if you were not tougher, stronger, and wilier or did not have the killer instinct, you are just a future victim. Having a 'killer instinct' gives you the advantage to survive when everything else is equal."

I knew so little about the man except what I had learned in the last twenty-four hours. It was obvious that Samael Amos has a "killer instinct" and has drawn blood and has killed men before. Not just men, but modern mountain men like him, who had skills and have been schooled in the way of the mountains - tough men. Maybe it was as simple as that in the "why" he was doing what he has done - proving he is the best. Just because righteousness was on my side did not mean I would come out a victor in any confrontation with a man like Amos. The fact of the matter was even though I had survival and mountain skills, the difference was that Amos had killed before and I had not.

Remembering the Polaroid of Amos I had taken from his cabin, I took it out and studied it once again. This time I noticed something I had not seen before and that was just to the right of Amos was part of a national park sign. Most of the park sign had been cut out of the photograph, but sure as I am sitting here it was a national park informational sign. Holding the photo closer, I could see a capitol "T" to the far left of the sign and nothing more. Knowing it probably meant absolutely nothing, I could not help but wonder if the "T" was a clue to Amos' hideout and lair. I had been studying the photo so hard that when Nickey Lynn spoke, it startled me. She spoke in a tone just above a whisper, "Why you look so depressed and gloomy over there, Dane? It seems to me I should be the one all depressed and gloomy."

CHAPTER 23

For the next four days Nickey drifted in and out of sleep as her body and mind started to heal from the brutal attack from Samael Amos. Each time Nickey was lucid enough, she looked for me even when her folks were in the room. Every time when she had woken, I would stand or sit while I was holding her hand so she could focus on me. In a voice barely above a whisper, she would crack some small joke as she held my hand. Humor was her way of dealing with the emotional turmoil that was evident in her eyes. I knew her body would heal before her mind, but I was confident in my Nickey Lynn and knew she was a fighter and in the end she would prevail over this new demon in her life. I had to support her to the best of my ability until I no longer saw the fear present in Mi Vida's eyes. I feared it would be a tough road for my love.

The hotel room set up for me and being paid by Grand County was only used to shower and clean myself up. Every night I slept in the reclining chair in Nickey's room in intensive care not wanting her to wake up even once without me being there.

Of course it was more than just my love that made me not want to leave her side - it was also guilt. With each passing day, I felt increasingly guilty and restless as the manhunt in Rocky Mountain National Park continued for Samael Amos. Sheriff Walker called every day with updates as he promised, and I could hear his frustrations as it became more and more clear that with each passing day that Amos had vanished without a clue. Samael Amos had become a ghost. The Sheriff also added that the only clues that Amos had been involved with the disappearances of Micah, Craig Dale, and the others were the drivers' licenses that were thumbtacked to the wall. Also in the investigation it was learned that Amos had no friends and had become an apparition to his family and never kept in contact with them. Tom didn't say it, but I knew it would not be long before they called off the manhunt - they had nothing to go on and he could no longer justify the expense.

Nickey was able to stay awake on Sunday only until halftime as the Denver Broncos took on the Houston Oilers down in Texas at the Astrodome. I was glad that Nickey had fallen asleep before the Broncos fell to three and two on the season as the Broncos quarterback Steve Ramsey only threw for 88 years as he and the other Broncos struggled against Dan Pastorini and the Oilers losing 17-3.

After the game I noticed it had started to snow as I looked out the window. Stepping up to the hospital window, I looked westward toward the mountains and the sky was dark, ominous, and uninviting over the Rocky Mountains. If it was snowing here, it was snowing harder in the high country and Rocky Mountain National Park. The wind and the snow would erase any trail or sign that could possibly be used in trying to track down Samael Amos. With a pressing sense of helplessness, I knew without a doubt that they would call the manhunt off today. That night as I watched the news at ten pm at the nurses' station, they confirmed that the search for Samael Amos was called off when fourteen inches of snow had fallen during the day in the search area within Rocky Mountain National Park.

There also was a short segment on the news about Grand County Sheriff Deputy Gene Sanford who had been killed by Amos and that he would be laid to rest the following Wednesday which was October 13th at the Grand Lake Cemetery. The cemetery was just a few miles northwest of Grand Lake and south of the entrance into Rocky Mountain National Park. I was thankful that the photo they used of Gene was a flattering one of him wearing his uniform as he rode a horse in the Grand Lake 4th of July parade the previous year.

The following day on Monday, Sheriff Walker called and his voice generated frustration and depression as he formally told Nickey and me that the search for Amos had been called off. The recent snow had put law enforcement agents in harm's way due to the declining weather. He also added that even with the use of dogs and helicopters, not once did they have a sighting or even a scent for the dogs to track. The sheriff thought Amos had escaped and slipped through the net that had been thrown up around the park. He wanted Nickey and me both to know that every law enforcement agency in the United States, Canada, and Mexico had been alerted and sent flyers on Samael Amos. They had also contacted an FBI profiler, and their assessment was that there was a high possibility that Amos had committed suicide once reaching the park after realizing the magnitude of his situation. As educated as the FBI profiler must surely be, he was wrong. The Ute Indian blood hastening in my veins told me that Amos was not dead and still within the boundaries of the park and in his mind probably more alive than he had ever been. Amos, the modern mountain man, had now reverted to the mindset of mountain men of old. He believed he was born 150 years too late and now he had stepped back in time so to speak. He now was no different than my ancestors dating back to my Grandfather Matt Lee. My gut was telling me that yes, he was still alive and roaming my mountains with an air of superiority. Amos had killed time and time again without ever being caught or until now not even suspected. He must feel that he was invincible as long as he stayed in the Rocky Mountains

The Rocky Mountain News this morning ran an article detailing the attack on Nickey and Gene; there was no mention of Micah, Craig Dale, and the others that were chronicled within the pages of the unfinished manuscript "The Daunting." They did give some details about Samael Amos. It would seem he was a native of Colorado and had attended Silver State Baptist, a parochial high school in Denver. According to the article Amos was a loner and played no sports and spent all of his available time up in the mountains. After high school Amos did a tour in Vietnam and was honorably discharged and then got a job with the park service presumably to be close to the only thing that mattered to him - the call of the wilderness.

Late that afternoon the hospital moved Nickey out of intensive care and into a regular hospital room so she could start some physical therapy. Her body it would seem was slowly healing and gaining strength, but her eyes still showed the fear of what happened and it broke my heart. I wanted to set things right in her world, but right now I did not know how to proceed.

Once Nickey was settled in with new IV drips in her arms, I sat down in the recliner in the room as she started to doze off. There was a magazine which I presumed was left by the previous occupant, and I picked it up out of boredom and was happy to see it was a Field and Stream magazine although over a year old. Thumbing through it, I found an article about Rocky Mountain National Park. The article was about good fishing areas within the park, and I read until I came to a photo of a sign. The sign was the typical photo of a park informational sign and it said, "Timber Lake 4.8 miles" with an arrow pointing presumably in the direction of the lake. Taking out the photo of Amos I had stolen from the cabin, I compared it to the photo in the magazine of the partial park sign and I realized without a doubt I was looking at the same sign in both photos. Samael Amos had been standing next to the Timber Lake sign when he had the grainy and yellowed Polaroid taken of him. Then it hit me like a ton of bricks that the Timber Lake trail that led to Timber Lake was one and the same from my reoccurring dream with grandfather. Standing up suddenly, I paced and tried to put two and two together and filter what information I had about the dream, the two photos, and Timber Lake.

Timber Lake was just west of Mount Ida and southeast of Jackstraw Mountain. Timber Lake trail was just like the park sign said and was 4.8 miles of moderate to difficult terrain from the trailhead for either hiking or riding horseback. Micah and I knew it well and would either hike or ride horses to fish the cold waters of Timber Lake. The Timber Lake trail curls south through an aspen and lodgepole forest accented by arnica, kinnickinnick, columbine and fallen trees. It rises steadily across a steep north to south hillside to a stream that feeds the Colorado River. Gaps in the forest offer partial views of the Never Summer Mountain range to the west. It would be a place that Micah would have gone by himself to fish since he knew the area well, as did I. There was now no doubt in my mind the trail in my dream was the Timber Lake trail! Samael Amos' lair and hidey hole was somewhere close to Timber Lake - It all came together, and I just knew it to be true!

My pacing the room like a caged animal had woken up Nickey Lynn, and she startled me when she asked in an almost scared voice, "Dane, what is wrong?"

As I turned toward Nickey with the magazine and the photo still held out in front, it took me several seconds to find my voice. "Nickey, I know where he is! I know where that son of a bitch Samael Amos is!"

Nickey Lynn was looking petite and frail from Amos' vicious and unhuman attack and her life and death struggle afterward, but there were still fighting and resolve in her eyes as she spoke in a voice still just above a whisper, "What? How could you possibly know, Dane?"

So I rushed quickly to her side still holding the Field and Stream magazine when I tripped over the hospital bed control cord and almost landed in bed with Nickey. After saving myself from falling into bed with her, I grabbed her hand and bent down to look in her eyes and once again, my heart was bleeding for the hurt that Samael Amos had caused the woman I loved. Lowering my voice to a whisper I said, "I know Nickey because of this" as I held out the magazine and showed her the photo of the Timber Lake sign in the park. Once I knew she had seen it, I laid down the magazine and then showed her the photo of Samael Amos standing next to this very same sign I had stolen from his cabin.

First a look of confusion and then worry crossed Nickey's face as I am sure she had thought I had lost my mind. Slowly she spoke again, "I guess I don't see the connection Dane on how that could mean he's still in the park. Sheriff Walker thought he had slipped out of the park before setting up the roadblocks and such."

Laying down the magazine, I said in a calm manner as not to sound as if I had gone off my rocker, "Sheriff Walker is wrong Nickey. Amos is at home in the park - the park is part of him. He would never leave it because he feels safe there, and it is his range. Just like a wolf or a mountain lion, he will travel but will always return to his lair. Also, the sheriff does not know about my reoccurring dreams with grandfather, the wilderness trail, and of

Micah lying dead with a knife in his chest. Grandfather was telling me the whole time where to hunt my enemy; I just didn't understand the sign and the message - until now! My mind always knew the wilderness trail in the dream was the key and the answer. It was not until I saw that photo of the Timber Lake sign that it all came together. A trail that Micah and I had often used. That son of a bitch is hiding out in some sort of a lair near Timber Lake."

Nickey's swollen and knife sliced face that showed confusion and worry before now showed understanding as she believed me before she spoke. "You need to call the sheriff and let him know, Dane."

Pulling up the chair, I sat down and scooted it closer to Nickey. "Can't do that, Nickey. No way in hell will the sheriff mount another expensive manhunt based on a photo in a year old magazine and a photo I stole from a crime scene. Plus, he does not know about my grandfather dreams and would think I was touched in my head if I told him. This is for me to finish and me alone, Nickey. Grandfather told me so; now I know what the dream was all about. This showdown with Amos or retribution is a reckoning for Amos and myself and no one else."

Bending closer to Nickey, I stated something that was burning in my Ute Indian blood, "I am going after him, Nickey. And for what Amos did to Gene, Micah, and you - he does not get to live - I am not bringing him back!"

Nickey's face showed not only the understanding, but it now also showed the determination that matched my own as she leaned so close to me that our lips almost touched. I could see the fire and fight in her eyes as they locked onto my eyes before she spoke. "I understand Dane, and I don't want you to bring him back!"

Having said that, I could still see concern and worry on Nickey Lynn's face so I asked, "I still see concern, so what else is on your mind, Mi Vida?"

A tear formed in Nickey's eye as she touched the stitches that held together the angry and swollen knife cut that Amos had afflicted on her face. "My face is flawed and will always be scarred. I worry you won't love me anymore!"

Slowly I reached up and gingerly touched the wound on her face and in reality I had not thought about it other than how much physical pain it caused Nickey. I had not thought about the emotional pain of disfigurement because to me it did not weigh in on how much I loved this woman. As several tears formed in my eyes, I knew no matter what I said now it would not be enough. But looking into her eyes, I had to say something. "Oh Nickey my love, in the beginning there is no denying that your physical beauty is what attracted me to you, because that is how it works. It was not before long in our relationship I got to see the beauty of your soul, and in the end that is what really matters. Nickey, I will always love you, no matter what, and that scar that will form will be a part of you and it does not matter, for my love for you is not measured in only physical beauty, but the whole package."

Saying that, I knew my words would not wash away her fears about the knife wound and eventually the scar and her face showed a frown so I added, "To be honest Nickey, I never really saw you as a '10' anyway and any scar will, of course, drop you down a point or so."

Nickey raised her eyebrows to go along with her now deepening frown, so I quickly added the rest, "You were always a '12' in my eyes so I guess now you will be an '11' still one point ahead of the rest of the beautiful women in the world."

Nickey's sulk disappeared rapidly and was replaced with an ever widening smile, and her eyes showed me her laughter as she said, "Dane, you have always been a smooth talker with the ladies, but sometimes you have your head up your butt. But as the Lord is my witness, I love you more each and every passing day."

The smile faded and the mope and apprehension returned as she spoke again, "Dane, after whatever happens with Samael Amos, you must return quickly to me. And when you do, we will never speak of him again. Promise me that!"

After kissing her gently on her lips and as I looked into her eyes as I pulled back, "I promise Mi Vida, I promise."

CHAPTER 24

The next morning after Nickey woke up, we discussed my leaving and going back to Grand County for Gene's funeral, and then I would push on into the park in my quest to locate Samael Amos.

Nickey understood the obvious danger I would put myself in, and the last kiss before I left lingered for what seemed a long time as Nickey Lynn's eyes glistened with tears. She held me tightly before she let me go and when I walked out of the hospital room, I could not find the courage to look back at her. I knew it was best that way, and I think Nickey knew it as well.

Before leaving Denver, I stopped at Gart Brothers sporting goods on Broadway to pick up some of the latest gear for winter survival. I was well prepared for travel in the mountains, but there were a couple of items I had been wanting to buy and now seemed like the right time to do so.

The first thing on my list was some new Sherpa aluminum snowshoes to replace my much heavier wooden snowshoes. The new Sherpa was much lighter due to the aluminum construction and were oval shaped. The second thing on my list was the brand new designed Snow Lion Polarguard Mummy sleeping bag which was a high performance synthetic stuffed bag. The Snow Lion used continuous fiber filament Polarguard insulation that kept warmth evenly distributed. The third item was a new Petzl headlamp.

As I was leaving Gart's, I ran through my mind the rest of my winter survival gear I had at home in Granby and felt I was more than ready for an extended stay in the high mountain cold and snow.

Before I left Nickey, one of the things we discussed was that I was taking both Thunder and Cochise with me into Rocky Mountain National Park. I would ride Thunder my Mustang mare because she was a tad larger, and I thought she could carry my weight in the cold and snow better than Cochise. I would use Nickey's Appaloosa gelding as a pack horse and backup if something should happen to Thunder. It had been some time since both horses had been on an extended excursion into the mountains and never once at the beginning of winter, but I felt they both were capable of the task.

After a seemingly long drive over Berthoud Pass and back to Granby, I spent most of the rest of the day with Thunder and Cochise, feeding them some grain and giving both a good currying as I rubbed them down getting them prepared for what lay ahead.

Once I got home, the house seemed gloomy and empty without Nickey Lynn, but I kept busy getting my gear and weapons ready before I called Nickey Lynn on the phone. Our conversation was strained somewhat because neither of us wanted to talk about what I was planning on doing, so we kept the conversation short and to the point. Hanging up the phone, I realized it would be some time before I would talk to Mi Vida again. There would be no phone booths where I was going.

After a quick dinner of two fried hamburgers, I lay down in bed and I quickly fell asleep.

The dream started this time at the Timber Lake trailhead and the sign showing the direction of the lake, and the distance of 4.8 miles was clearly visible this time. No more mystery of where the trail was. It was snowing, but I did not feel the cold as the horses and I moved eastward down the trail toward Timber Lake, and it was not long and grandfather appeared silently and ghosted out of the woods and stood before me as he said in a loud voice that surrounded me, "Step down Dane, we need to get your mind straight for the undertaking at hand."

Very little in the dream so far was the same this time except for the trail and grandfather. Confused, I stepped out of the saddle and my boots sank into six inches of undisturbed snow. There was a fallen tree on the side of the trail, and I took a seat after brushing off the snow as grandfather did the same. Grandfather took out the same knife and the same piece of aspen wood from the previous dreams, and he whittled as he looked at me. Grandfather looked into my soul with ageless and ethereal eyes. I felt my ancestors' blood as it quickened in my veins. It was at this moment I felt as if I had lived in another lifetime - a previous life back when my ancestors lived when your life counted solely on your skill with weapons, wilderness survival, and cunning. Where there was no law but that of nature and the tip of your knife. Grandfather knew he had my attention as he spoke with that "you better listen to me now" voice. "Dane, you have come far and the blood of these mountains, your Ute Indian heritage, and my blood run in your veins. In the battle ahead, you must set aside all that you have lived and learned from the society that has gone soft and let your instinct of the mountain man warrior take over and guide you. Don't think - just do! Feel the blood of your ancestors, for they will guide you in the quest before you. Courage above all things is the first quality of a warrior, and the Ute Indians were the most courageous warriors of the Rocky Mountains. It is important for you to understand that the way of the warrior is resolute acceptance of death; once you accept the fact it is do or die, is when the Ute warrior's heart will beat within your chest. You will know fear, for a true warrior is not immune to fear, but will fight on despite it. It is the nature of the Lee clan to be gentle, loving, and kind, but our enemy must know this. When it comes to protecting or seeking vengeance and justice for our friends, family, and our heart, they will know they should not have trifled with us since we are the most powerful and relentless mountain warriors they will ever know!"

Suddenly I woke up and looked at the empty bed next to me and thought about Nickey and the pain and misery Amos had caused Mi Vida as I rehashed what grandfather had told me in the dream about the Lee Clan being powerful and relentless warriors. I had self-doubt I could live up to that claim, but I sure as hell was going to try.

As I looked out through the window, the sun as yet had not made an appearance and it was doubtful from the look of the sky that it would today. The heavens were clouded, dark, gray, and somber on this morning, which seemed fitting in some ways since Gene was being laid to rest in the Grand Lake Cemetery. The rest of the morning I kept my mind focused and occupied as I double checked my wilderness survival gear and weapons for what I had to do after Gene's funeral.

Later, at the memorial service that was held at Hot Sulphur Springs Community Church for Gene, Sheriff Walker did a double take when I walked in. It was obvious he was not expecting me to be here, but instead to still be at Nickey's side in the hospital at Saint Anthony's. The media outside of Grand County that had descended into the area had trickled down to just a few reporters from Denver after the manhunt for Samael Amos had been called off. Gene's brother read the eulogy that was heartwarming and depressing at the same time as he relived the life of my friend and co-worker whose life had been taken way too early in life. There were the usual hymns you hear at most funerals, including my all-time favorite Amazing Grace. Each time I hear that old hymn it always fills my soul with a sense of purpose and knowledge that there is something else beyond this life. It was the same feeling I felt when I could feel my Ute ancestors that reached out from the forgotten past as they stirred my blood from time to time. Not all believe in God, spirits and ghost, but I do. I know that they are real.

After the memorial service in Hot Sulphur Springs, the hearse carried Gene's mortal remains as the rest of the churchgoers and I followed behind twenty-five miles to the Grand Lake Cemetery. The dark clouds of the day finally began to snow at the end of the graveside services, and I turned northward to look at the mountains of the Timber Lake area not more than a few miles away from this very spot that I was standing. My mind focused on the task ahead and the eventual showdown with Samael Amos. My mind was so focused on the not so far away Timber Lake that when Sheriff Walker spoke it startled me. "Sort of surprised to see you Dane, thought you would still be with Nickey."

Turning to look at my friend and boss, I found my voice and replied, "I came to see Gene off, but with your permission I still need more time off from work."

Sheriff Walker was not a dumb man by any means, and he knew from my demeanor that something was off kilter and he was yet to put a finger on it as he spoke again. "Not an issue Dane, take all the time you need. I spoke with the hospital today and they said Nickey is gaining strength and has started physical therapy. I reckon she could still use your support for a spell."

We had come to the crossroad of this conversation I would have rather avoided, but I looked Tom straight in the eye and with a clear and calm voice said, "Not going back to Denver, Tom; I am taking the horses and heading up into the park."

Sheriff Walker's face showed worry and concern and he stood silent for over a minute as he rolled it around some in his mind what I had said. "Dane, we had over a thousand men, eight dogs, and one helicopter looking for Amos for over a week. He is not there anymore or if he is, he is sure enough dead by suicide. There is nothing you can do that has not already been done. I do not think it is wise you go alone into the remote wilderness at the start of winter."

Even if I thought Tom would believe me that I knew where Amos was, I wouldn't tell him. This was for me to do now and to do alone. I must leave the civilized Dane Lee here and take what remained of him, which was controlled by his ancestral blood and the call of the mountains. The Ute spirits and my grandfather had spoken and had given me a quest and a trail to follow. My blood burned, and I could not deny my heritage. I turned back and looked north again toward Timber Lake before I spoke. "I understand and thank you for your concern, Tom. I reckon I am still going!"

CHAPTER 25

Tom, my friend and boss, hesitated but finally relented and granted me my wish of more time off. He knew in his heart that if he didn't, I would quit the sheriff's department and do it anyway. As Tom shook my hand, I could see in his eyes he thought I was making a terrible mistake. I probably was.

After the graveyard service I went through the motion of saying all the correct things to those that were in mourning from the grief of Gene's death as my mind was really focusing on the Timber Lake area and Samael Amos to the north. I faded when the others were not looking into the evergreen trees that surrounded the cemetery and waited until everyone had left; I wanted a few moments alone with Gene. After the last of family and friends that had come to the graveyard service drove off, I strolled to Gene's grave, and the two cemetery groundskeepers that had the task of burying my friend stepped aside to a respectful distance and bowed their heads silently as they gave me space and some time alone with Gene.

The stylish wooden coffin that carried the human remains of one of my best friends had already been lowered into the ground as I crouched and sat on the ground next to the grave Indian style, looking down into what now seemed a very deep abyss of a hole in the ground. I realized in my heart that the Gene that I knew was not in the coffin. His physical remains were but not his essence and soul. I could feel his presence and spirit all around me in this - his final resting place. Now looking skyward, I spoke to the wind and the mountains since I knew he was there now wandering the mountains with those that had passed on before him. "Well shit! I am sorry my friend I was not by your side when death came calling. Believe me, my pal, I would trade places with you if I could, but I can't since I still have a task to finish. Amos and death have taken your life. God now has your soul. In my mind I hold your memories; in my heart I hold your love. My faith knows we will meet again my friend. With God and the mountain spirits as my witnesses, I will avenge you Gene! I will avenge Micah and Nickey Lynn as well or I will die trying! That is my promise to you! That is my promise to all of you!"

Having said what I needed to say, I stood once again, and I knew my words were hollow if I did not carry through. My words did not mean jack shit as long as Samael Amos was still alive. I looked once again to the north where I knew Amos was hiding in the wilderness surrounding Timber Lake because that is where my ancestors and grandfather had showed me he was. Soon I would ride there for justice and a reckoning with a devil named Samael Amos.

Turning to leave, I remembered something, and I turned back toward Gene and his coffin and I reached inside my coat and produced the latest edition of "Mad" the magazine with the grinning cartoon caricature of Alfred E. Neuman on the cover. Just the thought of Gene reading this brought a smile to my face as I tossed the magazine on top of the coffin. "Brought you a present buddy to help you make the transition into the spirit world."

Just before I climbed into my county Blazer, I stopped and looked back at the two groundskeepers that were now hard at work burying my friend with good, clean and pure Rocky Mountain soil. In my mind and heart, I knew with what was still ahead of me, they might put me in the ground right beside my old friend.

The day was well past noon, so I decided to leave in the morning for the park. I would ride Thunder trailing Cochise from Granby to get them familiar with being back on the trail before it became more rugged in Rocky Mountain National Park. Plus, I wanted no one dropping the horses and me off or leaving my Grand County Sheriff's Blazer and horse trailer within the park. I wanted to ghost my way into the park and move like the mountain men of old - like Matt Lee my grandfather.

Driving back to Granby from the cemetery in Grand Lake, I did not listen to any music or the radio, for my mind was filled with remembering my dreams - the Timber Lake area, grandfather, Micah, Gene, and of course what had happened to Nickey Lynn. Once again, I doubted if I could bring justice to Amos, but in the end it did not matter since I had to try. My blood was on fire and it was now a part of me. It was as if my life before never existed and what was from this moment on down the trail not only the beginning of life as I knew it but also the end. I thought about what grandfather had told me in the last dream. *"It is important for you to understand that the way of the warrior is resolute acceptance of death."* I was okay with the realization that I may die in the mountains that were so much a part of my heritage and the Ute blood running its course through my veins. In the end a warrior's death may await me in the mountain snow and cold and my body may never be found. Looking out the Blazer window at the fast moving mountainside, I decided it was a good day, week, or month, and place to die. If fate chose me to die in this quest for retribution, the feeling I have is my ancestors and grandfather would be proud.

I spent the rest of the day grooming and graining the horses and looking after my gear and weapons. My pistol of choice was the same one I carried every day as a Grand County Sheriff's officer and that was an older 357 Ruger 3-screw Blackhawk. My 357 used to belong to my dad, and I did not know the year they manufactured it other than it was after 1962 and before 1973. My Blackhawk hammer had four distinct clicks that could be heard while it was brought back to full cock, which was characteristic of the Colts pistols. One had to free spin the cylinder for loading, and the hammer had to be placed at half-cock, another characteristic of Colts and older single action revolvers. Because the lock work was so similar to that of the Colt, the Ruger Blackhawk had three screws on the side of the frame just as the Colts did. How I knew my Ruger was built after 1962 was because it had "ears" to the top strap of the revolver around the rear sight which was not a feature of the gun before 1962. The holster I carried my 357 in was a simple tan leather affair and was well worn since I wore it almost every day. I also had gained the skill of a fast draw just as all the Lee mountain men had, dating all the way back to Matt Lee. My fast draw came from a lot of practice and had become almost as natural as pointing my finger. My rifle of choice was also the rifle of choice of the Grand County Sheriff's department, a 1974 Ruger mini 14. Ruger had shrunk M-14 7.62 service rifles into a more compact version that chambered a 223 shell. The Grand County Sheriff's department required us as officers to be proficient with the rifle and I was an excellent shot with it.

About six pm I called Saint Anthony's, and they connected me to Nickey Lynn's room and she answered on the first ring. At first our conversation was filled with anxiety and tension; we both knew in the back of our minds this might be the last time we ever spoke. After getting Nickey's physical update and how she was progressing with her physical therapy, I knew I had to end this call because I could hear my love as the tears started to flow. She was trying to be strong, but it was not to be. I finally said in a calm and clear voice, "Nickey I need to go. There is a lot I have to do before I am ready to leave in the morning. You need to know this before I hang up - there is not a minute, hour, or day that I do not think of you and the love we have shown each other. This love - our love - is what makes me breathe the air and soak in the sunshine. This morning was the hardest morning I have ever had to endure. I looked at your side of the bed and it was empty except that lingering smell of you that I love. It was at this moment when I realized it only takes seconds to say hello and forever to say goodbye. The easy part is for me to ride into battle; the hard part my love is leaving you behind. Whatever happens as I go face our one and only demon into the wilderness, just know that if I should die, my last thought will be of you! If fate smiles on my quest to bring justice to our enemy that has caused so much bloodshed and fear, then I shall ride like the wind back to you. Nickey Lynn Chavez - I LOVE YOU!"

There was silence on Nickey's end as my words sank in and just before Nickey hung up, she said as she chocked back her tears, "Do what needs to be done Dane, because I know it is you that has to bring this full circle. Come back to me soon Dane Lee, for you are my soulmate and love of my life!"

CHAPTER 26

My dinner that evening was a Swanson TV dinner of some undesirable mushy fried chicken, but it was food and protein, both of which I would need in ample supply in the days ahead. After I watched the evening news, there was no mention of Gene, Nickey Lynn, or of Samael Amos the man who had gotten away with murder of two of my best friends and had almost killed my woman. The world had moved on from Amos, and that was proof enough that any justice that needed to be done was for me to do alone.

The night went by with none of the dreams of grandfather's offering wisdom or advice. It was as if he knew I had all the information that was needed, and the task and now manhunt rested solely on my shoulders and no one else's.

Getting up before sunup and while dressing, I picked up my sheriff's badge from the bedside table and looked at it for a long spell realizing what I was planning on doing was not within the confines of the law. Modern law had no room for vengeance and revenge. I would ride into harm's way with no legal status other than what was righteous. I was placing my life and career in jeopardy and I was okay with that regardless of the outcome.

Laying my badge back down on the bedside table, I walked away to the kitchen to make some breakfast.

After I made a hearty breakfast of bacon and eggs and toast, the whole time I was wolfing down my chow and staring at the cook stove, my thoughts were of the past of when Nickey only dressed in a T-shirt and panties as she cooked my breakfast. It was an image that would forever be burned in my brain. My mind also wandered to her lingering kisses and my feeling of love for her. I had to bring it all full circle to get her home where she belonged. My heart had already decided if I survived Amos and the mountains, I was going to ask Nickey to marry me. Just the thought of asking her brought another smile to my lips and flutters to my heart and soul. I truly loved that woman more than life itself and needed her home, and I needed to survive; one was easier than the other.

Loading my gear, provisions, and weapons in the county sheriff's Blazer, I drove in silence to the horse property that Thunder and Cochise were at. After saddling Cochise, I positioned my all white saddle panniers over the saddle and loaded my gear and provisions into that. After I saddled Thunder and after placing my rifle in a scabbard that rode just below my right hand, I stepped in the stirrup and planted my butt in the saddle. My 357 rode easily in the holster as I reined Thunder toward the north and looked at the sky over Rocky Mountain National Park and the Never Summer Mountains.

After I gave Thunder a slight jab of my spur, she hesitated and looked back at Cochise as Nickey's horse was looking back at the sheriff's Blazer. It was as if they were both wondering where Nickey Lynn was as I spoke to them softly, "Listen up the both of you, Nickey is okay, but not able to ride this trail with us. She, of course, will ride in spirt and our hearts."

The sun had finally breached the top of the mountains to the east and was giving the sky an orange and blue hue that was breathtaking in its grandeur. There were clouds in the north, the direction of Rocky Mountain National Park and Samael Amos. The air was chilled on this autumn day as we began the ride of almost sixteen miles to the Rocky Mountain National Park entrance. My plan was to get there at dark and slide on past the gates and the highway as I ghosted into what would now be my hunting grounds.

The Trail Ridge Road was officially closed for the season due to the winter snow, but the gates and entrance booths may still be manned with some park rangers such as Sandee Adams as some hardy folks could still visit the Kawuneeche Valley on this side of the Continental Divide. People and especially the park rangers I wanted to avoid, so just like the name given by the Ute Indians to my Grandfather Matt Lee, I would become "Ghost."

By noon Thunder, Cochise, and I were riding the shore line of Shadow Mountain Lake, and the surprised look on the fishermen we passed was more than humorous. I wanted to avoid riding down Highway 34 as much as I could, but that was proving difficult because since the days of my grandfather and ancestors, the land all had become privately owned and they had installed fences to protect the privacy of the owners. I could only imagine back in the days when only the Ute Indians and the mountain men rode these trails how peaceful and free the people of the mountains must have felt. In the afternoon I rode past the turnoff toward Grand Lake and still heading north, I faded into the woods on the west side of the road as I got closer to the entrance of the park which was the beginning of Kawuneeche Valley.

Kawuneeche Valley was also known as Coyote Valley. The word Kawuneeche means coyote in my ancestors, the Utes' and the Arapahoe Indians' languages. The marshy valley follows south to north along the beginning of the Colorado River and is located on the west side of the Continental Divide of Rocky Mountain National Park. Wolves are said to be extinct in the valley and Rocky Mountain National Park, but there had been rumors of sightings in the last few years as nature tries to reclaim its own territory. Of course the park had abundant wildlife in the form of mule deer, mountain lions, elk, bobcats, raccoons, rabbits, bighorn sheep, and other critters.

The bighorn sheep population was making a slow, but steady increase. In the mid-1880 and early 1900's, the bighorn population declined rapidly. Initially, market hunters shot bighorn by the hundreds to receive higher payments for the prized horns and meat. When ranchers moved into the mountain valleys, they altered important bighorn habitat and introduced domestic sheep. The domestic sheep carried scabies and pneumonia, which proved fatal to large numbers of bighorn sheep. By the 1950's it was estimated that only 150 big horns still roamed the Never Summer Mountains. Since it is illegal to hunt within the park's boundaries nowadays, their population has increased as evidenced by the bighorn tracks I was trailing as four of them seemed to be taking the same trail as Thunder and Cochise and I were riding.

Riding into the slight northern wind, I could see off to the east the entrance booths and gates, and they seemed abandoned as the sun started to dip behind the mountains to my west. Night comes quickly in the mountains, and we rode on for another mile in the dark until finding a suitable place to camp for the evening sheltered in the trees from the mountain winds.

The first order of business was to see to the horses and their needs first. Stripping them of their saddles and panniers, I took the time to rub them down thoroughly with a wooden curry comb. Both were loving the extra attention being showed them and although patient with me as I groomed the other horse, the one not being groomed stomped his hoof and snorted until I turned my attention back to him. They were acting like kids, and I gave them a treat of a pinch of sugar each. After graining the horses, I left them not hobbled for the night as they pawed through the snow for any grass or roots they could scrounge up.

I gathered up kindling and wood for a fire and used stick matches that had been dipped in wax, and a warming and cook fire took blaze. Micah was the first one when we were kids that showed me how simple it was to make waterproof matches. I always carried flint as my ancestors and grandfather used to do to make a fire in the old ways, but as long as I had the means to make a campfire more easily, I would use it, thinking grandfather would not mind. As I went about my camp chores, my mind was adrift thinking about the book "The Daunting," Craig Dale, Gene, Micah, the others in the book, and of course Nickey. Moving closer to the Timber Lake area, I would have to void my mind of any distractions of the past and focus on the present to stay alive. Starting tomorrow the manhunt for Samael Amos would start in earnest.

Beef steak and fried taters were on the menu for my supper this evening and just like Thunder and Cochise wanting a sugary treat, there were several cans of pears in my provisions. I loved drinking the syrup that the pears came in.

As the early evening wore on, the air got colder, the sky clouded over, and the stars above became hidden as the night mist moved in. If it was not for the reason I was here in the first place, I would be soaking up the peace and harmony in this setting with being one with nature with a nice warm fire by which to warm my chilled hands. The horses did not seem alarmed; they seemed content. The ears and nose would be a big advantage as I got closer to Timber Lake and Amos. I knew full well the ears and noses of Thunder's and Cochise's keen senses would help warn me in case of danger as mine got accustomed to the wilderness.

Rolling up in my new mummy sleeping bag, I closed my eyes and fell asleep to the eerie sound of an elk bugling in the distance.

CHAPTER 27

Several snowflakes melted on my face, which brought me to a full awaking. After I quickly glanced to the horses and after several seconds had passed, the feeling of relief came over me as they were still content this morning - meaning we were all alone - just us and the wilderness.

My body ached from sleeping on the ground and although I was in tremendous shape, it would take several nights of sleeping this way before once again getting accustomed to the hard ground and the coldness of the night. Standing slowly, I tried to ease my muscles into moving as to try to warm them up for the day ahead. Bending down and stirring the ashes from last night's campfire and after finding some still glowing embers, I stirred them to the top to feed them on the oxygen it needed to make a fire. Once a small flame started to dance and after adding kindling and before long some larger logs, the smell and the snap and crackle of a decent size warming and cook fire came to life.

The sky was lighter as the morning was approaching from the east, but the morning sun with its warming rays was hidden behind the dark clouds in the sky above stretching as far as I could see over the Continental Divide.

It was snowing here in Kawuneeche Valley, a silent and easy snow with quarter size snowflakes that drifted back and forth lazily as they descended to the ground. There was zero wind this morning, and the air was crisp and cold and in the stillness of the morning, one could hear evergreen and aspen trees moan and creak as the temperature dropped and played havoc with the wood and tree sap.

My senses were keener than most modern men, but it still takes a full day or two in the wilderness to get what my dad used to call "mountain man's awareness." In the days gone by during my Grandfather Matt Lee's time, not having this awareness would get you killed in a heartbeat. This was now true for me since the man whom I hunted would surely have his. Mountain man awareness was the natural ability to focus on all things in the wild and nature. Most people walk in the woods and deep timber and miss 90% of the reality that surrounds them. They do not hear the music of the forest, and they cannot see the struggles of life in nature that are before them. Society and technology had made man soft in the old ways of the Rocky Mountain frontier. To survive here in the high mountain winter, you had to have a gut instinct, mountain man's awareness, and in my case a killer instinct. My enemy would have all this - which would make him a deadly adversary. It was now do or die!

Still had one fresh beef steak and a half dozen chicken eggs in my supplies for my breakfast this morning, so it should be a good start of the day. Fearing my eggs had frozen during the night, I was pleasantly surprised when they were not and after searing and grilling my steak, I fried the chilled, but not frozen eggs over the campfire.

While savoring my breakfast, I thought back to my youth spent here in this park and these mountains and could not help but think of my dad, and his dad, and Micah. Micah was the first one that introduced me to the writings of John Muir. John Muir the naturalist had many quotes that spoke to me and this one is a favorite of mine. *"In every walk with nature one receives far more than he seeks."* Having read all of John Muir's writings, I felt at times he spoke only to me. The Rocky Mountains were my home and will forever be, and there was no doubt in my mind about that.

After I saddled and packed the panniers on Thunder and Cochise, the thoughts about the next leg of this manhunt, Timber Lake took over my thinker. Timber Lake trail was a two days' ride from here on horseback and none of it very difficult terrain. The lake itself was only 4.8 miles up that trail from Trail Ridge Road. My gut instinct, my dreams, and the photo I had taken from Amos' cabin told me this is where I should begin my search for Amos.

Before stepping into the stirrup, I checked my Mini 14 to make sure it was fully loaded as well as my 357 Ruger six shooter. Once starting north this morning toward the Timber Lake trail, I had to consider myself in hostile territory.

Drifting toward the north, we made our way through the evergreens and aspens as I led Cochise with a rope tethered to the back of my saddle on Thunder. The aspen trees here in the park had lost all of their leaves and looked bare and lonely. It continued to snow, but there was a hint of blue above the clouds so I knew it would not last long on this day. The accumulation so far was only about two inches of new snow.

Trying to stay away from Trail Ridge Road and Highway 34 and stay in the timber, I followed along the Colorado River as it followed the Green Mountain Trail. The trail at this point was fairly level although muddy from the recent snow and not difficult for Thunder and Cochise; it was actually a very pleasant ride. At ten in the morning it quit snowing and at noon the temperature had risen to about forty-five degrees with the sun breaking through the clouds. Looking due east, I could see the top of Green Mountain and occasionally through the trees the road signs of Trail Ridge Road that was in between the horses and me and Green Mountain.

At mid-afternoon I left the banks of the Colorado River as it took a sharp bend straight west for two miles before it meandered back north. Reining Thunder in the correct direction, we started to follow a tributary of the Colorado River called Onahu Creek. Onahu Creek flowed north to south into the Colorado River. Stopping for a spell at the end waters of Onahu Creek, the horses were getting their fill, and I ate a half pound of beef jerky and drank a full canteen of cold water. After refilling my canteen and stepping back into the saddle, I gave Thunder her head and some rein and once gain we moved out - slowly. Being in a hurry was not in the mountain man makeup. One had to take the time checking for signs and tracks of anyone else moving through the woods that was also being cautious. Samael Amos would have to be living off the land and that meant he had to be moving and hunting for food within the park's boundaries. So far the only sign and tracks I had seen were not of man, but of many deer and elk that were more than abundant within the park.

More or less following Onahu Creek as I headed north moving more in a straight line rather than the creek as it zigged and zagged along the Kawuneeche Valley floor, I still had not run across any people, which was my plan. It would not behoove me to have any reports back to the Grand County Sheriff's Department of a man riding horseback trailing another horse and armed to the teeth. If such a report was made, Sheriff Walker would know it was me, but in case he had doubts he might have to send officers to check on this mysterious rider. It was not in my scope of plans having to explain to a couple of sheriff's deputies and friends of mine what I was doing. I stayed off the main trails and roadways as I continued toward the Timber Lake area.

The sun settled down behind the western horizon as Onahu Creek passed under a small bridge on Trail Ridge Road, and Thunder and I, with Cochise trailing, traversed over the top of the bridge as the trail and the creek went from west to east. I rode on for another thirty minutes putting some distance between the horses and myself and the paved road before finding a suitable place to camp that provided shelter from the wind and with plenty of fresh water from the banks of Onahu Creek.

After unsaddling and unpacking the horses, I saw to their needs before my own and once satisfied that they had been well taken care of, I started a fire to fry up bacon and beans for my supper tonight. As the flames danced and made eerie shadows that swayed in the circle of light on the evergreen trees that surrounded my camp, I watched the burning red-hot embers of the fire as they floated lazily above the fire until they cooled and turned black into cold ash then floated away, and my mind pondered about Samael Amos the man.

Until now everything that the Grand County Sheriff's office and I had done was a reaction to the fast changing events regarding the fugitive park ranger. Amos, in fact, had killed Gene and tried to kill Nickey Lynn, and there was no question that this could be proven in a court of law. More than likely what could not be proven was he also killed Craig Dale, Micah, and the others that Dale had written about in his book "The Daunting." Amos seemed to be physically fit and fit the mold of a mountain man from days gone by, but what was not known was what he was like as a person. What made him tick—what made him do the things he has done?

It was obvious from walking around his cabin he was a loner and that he was more than self-efficient and wanted nothing from another individual. It seemed to me that he was not capable of what a normal person would call love. Obviously I was not schooled in the ways of a shrink or any school book learning in the ways of the human condition, but I was adept at observing people and had a knack for understanding what motivated most of mankind. My Ma used to say I was an "old soul" - meaning someone that had lived countless lives before this one and had gained insight in recognizing good and evil. There was no doubt in my mind that the man I was hunting was pure unadulterated evil.

CHAPTER 28

I woke up to darkness with no cloud cover, and the stars were shining and twinkling as they can only do at this altitude. Even as a little kid, I had fallen in love with the light that the stars above rained down on me and to never be fearful of the night. Looking at the position of the moon, I realized it was only about midnight and something had awakened me. The fire was all but out and gave off only a very faint orange glow from the dying embers as my eyes adjusted to the low light. All my senses were working overtime as they became one with the darkness and the stillness of the night. Thunder was close enough I could see her out of the corner of my eye, and she seemed to be content with no alarm, but looking to the east, I heard from that direction what had awoken me.

The timber wolf was far away in the distance, but his howl pierced the nightfall and became music to my ears and had woke me up. Some say wolves are no longer within the Rocky Mountain National Park's boundaries, but I knew otherwise. There was so much unexplored remote wilderness here for anyone that knew the mountains to say for certain the wolf had disappeared from Rocky Mountain National Park. From time to time I had viewed wolves in the distance as they viewed me with their intelligence on display for me to see. They were cunning, mighty hunters, and misunderstood by the public at large. The timber wolf was beautiful, graceful, wild, and the epitome of freedom. On this night knowing soon I would face life or death, I felt a kinship with that distant timber wolf. Unlike the wolf though, my heart was ruled by two moons in this wilderness setting - one that beckons me into the night as a savage beast - the other one calling me home to be at Nickey Lynn's side. I knew I had to give into the savage part of me to survive what was coming…soon.

After several minutes the timber wolf in the distance was silent and once again sleep overcame me. Grandfather, the old mountain man and my ancient angel, was silent as the wolf for the rest of the night. It would seem grandfather had no more advice or cryptic messages for me about Samael Amos.

Mi Vida, Nickey Lynn did however appear in my dream, and my heart fluttered to the beat of loving her. In this dream she was facing the sun with the Rocky Mountains in the background and her face had not been scarred by the knife of Samael Amos. Nickey seemed almost angelic, carefree, happy and content. Even in my dreamlike state I wondered if this vision of the woman I loved had some hidden ominous meaning, and I worried whether she was okay. In the dream the sun got brighter to the point I could no longer see Nickey's face and when the bright light faded, so did the image of Nickey. The dream woke me up for several minutes and as I watched the stars, I thought about my woman all alone in Denver still at the hospital, and now I had doubt if I had made the right decision to come here looking for Amos.

The sky had a hint of blue the next time I woke, and I looked quickly to the horses and they were at ease with their surroundings. As I sat up and stirred the ashes, I found some still hot embers and in short order had a warming fire at this beginning of this late autumn morning.

After a quick breakfast of fried bacon and beans rolled up in a warm tortillas, I made Thunder and Cochise ready for the day ahead. Checking the loads in my 357 and my Mini 14, I felt I was ready for the trail.

Placing the Mini 14 in the scabbard on Thunder's saddle, I holstered my Ruger and then pulled it out quickly in a fast draw. My Ruger slid easily and fast into my hand. I knew I was not as fast with my handgun as my ancestors were in the old days when being fast on the draw was a necessity, but I felt I was fairly fast as any modern man could possibly be. It was yet to be determined if being a quick draw with my Ruger would be the deciding factor if I lived or died in my upcoming encounter with Amos.

Once I was firmly planted into the saddle, I looked eastward as the sun finally broke the horizon over Sprague Mountain and Nakai Peak. For several minutes I basked in the glory of a Rocky Mountain burnt orange sunrise knowing if all went badly for me that this sunrise could be one of the last few I ever saw. Giving Thunder rein and her head, we once again followed Onahu Creek for another mile or so until we came to a "Y" in the small creek. Leaving the creek behind, the horses and I headed due north with Highway 34 and Trail Ridge Road two miles to my west toward the Timber Lake trail.

The air was cold enough to see my breath, and the evergreen trees moaned with the coldness as their wood and sap constricted even more. This sound that the trees made in late autumn and early winter was eerily beautiful and probably would send chills down the spines of those that had never experienced it. It was a sound I was accustomed to, and it sounded like home to me and the blood of my ancestors rushing through my veins.

As we ambled north, there was a dusting of new snow on the trail and it was easy to see the tracks of the deer and the elk as they moved about in their quest of living their lives in the high Rockies.

Hearing the sound of a magpie and then a crow, I tried to locate their whereabouts in the back woods. The crow found me and landed on an evergreen tree limb in front of me not more than ten feet away. I pulled back on Thunder's reins and brought her to a halt.

The crow's ebony feathers shimmered in the early morning light and almost seemed surreal. Crows just like this one were etched deep into Ute Indian mythology as a powerful spirit animal. It was handed down to me by my dad and my granddad that the crow knew all the mysteries of life and death and that they foretold of impending death. This Ute belief had been handed down to them from those that walked these mountains before them all the way back to Grandfather Matt Lee also known as Ghost and my Grandmother Walk With Ghost. Now, as I studied the black as night crow, the mysterious crow studied me and I knew this belief was not a legend or tall tale - that it was in fact true. Something sent this crow to give me guidance or show me the way - which one I was not sure of yet. I had no doubt that its presence here was also a foretelling of death to come. Only time and fate would answer if it was Samael Amos' death or my own.

For ten minutes the black crow and I had a meeting of kindred spirits before it flapped its wings and flew due north in the same direction I was heading as if he was showing me the trail I should follow. With an almost primitive feeling, I gave Thunder her head and the reins as we moved northward.

At midday I could see the snow-covered tops of Stone Peak and Mount Julian in the eastern horizon. The sky had turned gray as storm clouds moved in overhead and seemed to race south from the north and had the look of snow. As soon as the clouds showed up, the temperature fell and before too long it was below freezing, and I had to reach back into the saddlebag to produce gloves and full face white as snow balaclava.

Seeing movement out of the corner of my eye to the east, I pulled back on Thunder's reins and brought her and Cochise to a halt. I slowly took the glove off of my right hand to free it up in case I needed to pull my pistol or rifle. Concentrating on the evergreen tree line to the east, I slowly scanned the tree line looking for the movement again. All of my senses were on heightened alert as I watched and listened for anything out of kilter in the woods. The shadows of the trees were not long since it was just past midday, and my mind wanted me to believe it was only a shadow that had momentarily crossed my peripheral vision. I was close enough to Trail Ridge Road to the west that if there had been any vehicles on it, I would hear them as well, but the road was hushed and silent. My gut instinct was turning knots in my stomach, and I knew who or what I had seen was dangerous.

Ten full minutes I sat in the saddle and watched; Thunder and Cochise were starting to get nervy with me and started to toss their heads slightly and stomp their hooves. Not seeing anything again, I gave Thunder rein and continued north. As we moved ever so cautiously toward Timber Lake, I could not shake the feeling that someone back in the dark timber was observing the horses and me.

CHAPTER 29

As I moved northward vigilantly, my mind was focused and my eyes were tracking the tree line to the east looking for any movement again. The shadows, as the day grew longer, seemed to silently stalk me as they moved with the sun. When Micah and I were youngsters and found ourselves alone in the woods, we in our minds were mountain men and fearless - fearless except for the tree shadows. My dad used to spin tales of the Ute Indian spirits, ghost stories, and old poems at night around the campfire to entertain Micah and myself. One poem in particular always stuck with us, and it was called simply "Shadows." Riding Thunder on this day as the shadows of the trees moved along with us, I was flooded by memories of the poem I knew by heart and endlessly recited in my head.

Darkness of the night, the hour is late,
Shadows begin their dance, start to skate.
Full moon hidden behind dark clouds,
Shadows creep, ever growing dark shrouds.
Darkening shadows speak of increasing doom,

Swear the air chilled as cold as a tomb.
As a young lad, learned about shadows, beware,
Nothing stops them, not even the Lord's Prayer.
Apparitions jump from tree to tree,
As darkness and shadows begin to circle me.
Lost in the woods and vestiges to be feared,
Distance, in the distance an orange glow did appear.
Faster and faster as I approached the flickering light,
Shadows falling behind, during this full moon night.
Voices, laughter, the smell of a campfire,
Closer to the fire, the shadows begin to expire.

It was silly of course, but just thinking of the poem, brought some wonderful memories of Micah. Whenever I heard or thought of the word "shadows," my mind drifted back to Micah.

Based on the position of the sun in the sky, it was roughly three in the afternoon when I cut across the Timber Lake Trail. Pulling back on Thunder's reins, I brought her and Cochise to a standstill. Looking westward down the trail, I knew that Trail Ridge Road and Highway 34 were about a mile in that direction as was the sign in the photo with Samael standing next to it that I had taken from Amos' cabin. The sign in the photo proclaimed Timber Lake 4.8 miles was on the west side of this trail meaning that Timber Lake was east of me 3.8 miles. Looking eastward, I knew this trail well, for Micah and I used to fish Timber Lake several times a summer. I recognized this trail looking east, of course, but now it seemed different as the visions from my grandfather dreams came back to me. I was abruptly overwhelmed with sadness and grief, so much in fact, I had to stop myself from crying out loud. If I had ever doubted the dreams and especially the ones showing that Micah was killed here on this trail, that doubt vanished as my gut and instinct told me it was in fact true. Remembering the dreams now as if a motion picture show was playing in my head, I felt I had ridden to the exact spot that Micah had been stabbed to death. Stepping off of Thunder, I crouched Indian style and touched the ground and felt the energy of this very spot as it electrified my arm and flooded my brain. No doubt whatsoever - Micah had died here. Something or someone beyond this life had brought me to this exact spot - this I also knew to be true. Trying not to cry, but the tears slowly forming anyway, I felt Micah's presence here in this spot – his essence and spirit. My feeling was that Micah's apparition ghosted these trees and this trail waiting for the justice my best friend so deserved. There was no way in a court of law that it could be proven that Micah had been killed here over four years ago by Amos since there would be no evidence, for the passage of time had been so long. This journey, this manhunt was not about justice in the eyes of the law. It was about justice in what was right. Some may call it vengeance and the more I thought about it, that was a good word as well, but to me it felt more like a reckoning.

Gathering my wits, I stood up still holding the reins of Thunder and looked in the direction of Timber Lake, and that sense that someone was watching me felt stronger than ever. I pulled my Ruger, and it slipped easily and quickly into the palm of my hand, and I made sure it was fully loaded and ready in case I would need it. Holstering my 357, I stepped into the stirrup and got myself settled back into the saddle and looked once more at the ground where I believed Micah had been murdered. I gave Thunder her head and the reins and with a slight jab of my right spur, we moved slowly eastward following the trail toward Timber Lake over three miles in the distance.

By the time I reached Timber Lake, the sun and its warmth had already dropped behind the Never Summer Mountains to the west. As always darkness came early during the winter in the high mountains, bringing the chilled air of the night. My breath was visible as I breathed in and out as I unsaddled the horses, and by the frost that was building on the evergreen needles, I knew it was going to be a cold night.

My first task was to take care of the horses, and I spent considerable time using a curry comb on them. During this grooming of Thunder and Cochise, something seemed different. They were more skittish, and their eyes darted back and forth as if they were searching the surrounding darkness as if they knew something was amiss. Ever since we cut the trail toward Timber Lake, a sense of uneasiness had come over me, and the horses could sense that as well. My demeanor had put them on edge, and they could sense and feel as I did that something evil lived here. My gut was telling me that Amos and his lair were close and that he knew I was here as well. As I fed some grain with a pinch of sugar to both horses, that sinking feeling that someone was watching the horses and me was overpowering, and I didn't need grandfather in a dream to tell me it was Samael Amos.

What my next move was I didn't have a clue; fate and very little evidence had brought me to this point - this spot in the wilderness. This manhunt was just like a poker game, and I was waiting to draw my next card. Until picking up that card, I would not know if fate had dealt a winning hand or not. One thing was for sure this hand was being played to the end, and there would be no folding.

My gut told me Amos was close even though he probably did not have any idea if I was the law or not. Even if Amos had seen me around Grand County and had the wherewithal to put it together that I was the undersheriff, for most of the day if he was indeed watching my movements, he had not seen my face since I had been wearing my balaclava to ward off the cold.

I was convinced that my enemy already knew that I was here, and the thought of not having a fire for the night was dismissed, so I gathered enough stones to make a ring for a campfire. It was not long before there was a sizable cook fire for the night and some bacon and beans were frying. With some store bought tortillas, I made bacon and bean burritos for my supper and washed them down with a half of a canteen of very cold water.

The horses had moved closer to the fire this night than they had the evening before, and I think they felt the woods surrounding us were suspicious and they needed to be close to me as well. It was comforting to me as well knowing I had the ears, eyes, and sense of smell to warn me in advance of danger.

After supper I slipped the Ruger under Thunder's saddle that I was using as a makeshift pillow and kept my black handled buck knife within reach as well. Sleep was uneasy and I woke several times throughout the night, trying to hear anything out of the ordinary but hearing nothing but the winter sounds of the forest and then falling back to an edgy sleep.

Waking before dawn, I ate a cold breakfast of beef jerky and tortillas and drank a full canteen of water. Even as nervy as I was with my surroundings, my first thought of the day was of Nickey Lynn, and I wondered how she was making out in her healing process. If Samael Amos had not entered our lives and since today was Sunday, Nickey and I would have spent part of our day watching on television the Denver Broncos take on the despicable Oakland Raiders. Nickey despised the head coach of the Raiders John Madden with a passion. It would have been a fun day hating on the Raiders, but here I was freezing my ass off in the Rocky Mountains, and Nickey was recuperating at Saint Anthony's in Denver - all because of Amos.

My plan for the day was to ride around Timber Lake and to look for a sign of anyone moving about in the area. There would be critter tracks, of course, but I was looking for the tracks of a man - a lone man - named Amos.

Cochise was the first horse I got ready for the day and after fitting her with the panniers, I saddled Thunder and after tightening the cinch, I saw momentarily a flash of light over the top of the saddle and off to the east. A flash of light that would emit off of a pair of binoculars or possibly…a rifle scope.

CHAPTER 30

Looking once again over the saddle, I saw nothing in the east except trees and morning shadows. Whoever was watching me had slipped up momentarily and gave away their position. The only way into this area surrounding Timber Lake was the trail I was on, and there had been no tracks of a man or a horse. Whoever I saw has been here since before the last snow. My gut was telling me it was Samael Amos. He had not committed suicide as the FBI profiler wanted us to believe nor had he fled the area to other parts unknown as Sheriff Tom Walker believed. He had stayed where he felt safe.

Acting as if I had not seen that flash of light, I stepped into the stirrup and planted my butt firmly in the saddle. For the next few minutes, the tension built within my body as I waited for the shock of being shot out of the saddle. I was banking on the notion that Amos was not that type of serial killer and that sniping someone from a distance was not in his game plan. Using his knife to kill Gene and attack Nickey told me he liked to kill up close. It made it more personal and satisfying to him. My thought was that Amos believed he was invincible and that he was stronger, smarter, and more savage than anyone he chose to be his opposition.

The more I thought about it, the men in Craig Dale's book "The Daunting" - Bryan Amen, Jerry Toney, Randy Weems, Shawn Lord, Kevin Kyriss, and Micah and Craig Dale himself would never have known they were being stalked by a killer. As much as Amos liked to think he was master of the woods and his domain, stalking and killing men that did not know they were being hunted did not differ from shooting a deer from a hundred yards. I was different in that regard and even though I had never personally met him, I knew somewhat of his makeup as a killer. The other difference was I knew this was a game of life and death and only one of us would make it out of the wilderness alive. Micah, Craig Dale, and the others from the book would not have known this.

My next move was to draw him in close with him thinking I was not aware of his deadly intentions. For now, I was at a loss on how to do that. This whole ride for justice and a reckoning had been on gut instinct alone, and it would also determine the final outcome of what was to be in that manner. Thinking of my Grandfather Matt Lee and of the others with whom I shared blood and a kinship down through the years, I believed gut instinct was how they would have done it - the mountain man way.

Now the thought crossed my brain pan, as the horses and I moved to explore the banks and the trails back and forth from Timber Lake, that I should stalk the stalker. If I could cut the trail to Samael Amos' lair today, I would tonight after the sun goes down try to surprise him there. At this moment in time, he did not know who or what I was or that I even knew about his presence, and that was my one and only advantage. My motivation to kick in my killer instinct would be to remember Gene and Nickey as they lay bleeding and dying in front of the Amos cabin in Grand Lake. Those visions have never left me, and my ancestors' blood of Matt Lee and of the Ute burned within my veins as did the savage part of my heritage. I had to let go of the soft and civilized part of my inner self and become the savage of my forefathers. It was the way it was meant to be.

Moving with caution and keeping all of my senses alert, I thought about Timber Lake itself. It was a typical small high mountain lake that had the best fishing for cutthroats in late June and early July. On this October day the lake was partially covered with ice, and it would not be long before the ice covered the entire lake. The Timber Lake trail stopped here at the lake at 2000 feet below Mount Ida which was part of the Continental Divide and if I remembered correctly, was at about 12,800 feet in altitude. Bringing Thunder and Cochise to a halt, I viewed all that was around me; it was a diverse setting of streams, dry meadows, boggy meadows, moist and dry forest, lakeshore and tundra. Previously in my trips here, there seemed to be an abundance of elk, deer, and on two different occasions, bears. Most of the bigger wildlife and game had probably moved down to lower elevations with the onslaught of winter blowing down from the north. Since being this close to timberline the trees were scattered further up the slopes from the lake and from being here previously, I knew there was a flat summit above almost on top of the divide where there was a smaller lake called Julian Lake. I did not think Amos' lair would be near Julian Lake, for there was no shelter from the trees since there were none and the snow level could in the dead of winter reach up to thirty or forty feet. It was not a place I would want to winter in. My guess is that he would have sought to set up his camp closer to the inlet that feeds Timber Lake called Timber Creek. It was high enough that no one would be foolish enough to come here during the winter but low enough to have shelter from the wind and plenty of wild game to hunt for his food.

Moving south along the edge of Timber Lake, I crossed Timber Creek about mid-morning, which also had ice formed on its edges, but was still flowing a trickle of fresh cold creek water into the lake. At this junction I let Thunder and Cochise get their fill of water as I topped off my canteens. Standing up, I scanned the surrounding hillsides looking for any movement and about a half mile south, I could see what looked like a small cave just above some evergreen trees on the hillside. After retrieving my binoculars from my saddle bag, I took a closer look. It was indeed a small cave; I tried to steady my arm while watching it for several minutes and once for a fleeting second I thought I saw a wisp of smoke coming from the entrance. After ten more minutes of observation, I never again saw anything that might resemble smoke.

Hanging my binoculars around my neck, I climbed back into the saddle and gave Thunder her head and some rein and moved out to get a closer look at the cave. Stopping several times, I would look at the cave and then back to where I had camped last night, seeing that my camping spot would have always been observed from the cave. I had no illusions that Amos didn't know exactly where I was. The cave was a perfect place to detect any comings and goings from the trail coming in from Trail Ridge Road and the more I ran it through my thinker, it would be the perfect place to sit out the winter in relative comfort. You would have flowing water from the creeks most of the winter and when it froze, you could melt snow, have plenty of firewood, and have easy access to wildlife to hunt.

My bet was the cave was well stocked because a man who was a park ranger would have plenty of time and access to secure his lair in such a manner if he ever had to flee. He also would have had plenty of time to bring in provisions. After killing Gene and almost killing Nickey, Samael Amos had fled to the only place he would have felt secure. All I had to do was cut any trail or sign of Amos coming and going to the cave and then find a place to wait it out until dark.

Thunder and Cochise seemed to be on edge as well; they must sense the danger that was emitting from the cave and the surrounding woods as I did.

Just before noon I found what I was looking for – a well trampled trail with several boot tracks in the snow just fifty yards below the cave that led to the edge of Timber Lake. Samael Amos had made a mistake; he had been using the same trail repeatedly because he thought no one was looking for him anymore. Wanting him to think it was a game trail I had stumbled on in case he was still watching me, I rode over his trail without stopping and kept moving south at the slow pace the horses and I had been moving.

A plan of attack formulated in my mind that I would ride a quarter of a mile and find a suitable place to camp. After making camp, I would eat and wait until dark and then ghost my way like my ancestors back to the cave – Amos' Lair. My mind had already focused in on what I might expect once I confronted Amos. It had to be quick and deadly on my part, for Samael Amos had already proven that he was one tough son of a bitch.

They say if you hear the report of a rifle shot, it was not meant for you and that was true in this case as the sickening sound like a bullet hitting a watermelon flooded my ears and senses. Then I heard the sound and echo of the rifle as Thunder stumbled once, then twice after being shot in the chest.

CHAPTER 31

It took a couple of seconds for my mind to realize that the son of a bitch had shot Thunder as she stumbled a third time and then her front legs started to slowly buckle. Then she collapsed all the way onto her belly, and I stepped off her and while gaining my footing, I drew my Mini 14 rifle out of the scabbard. Then two more shots rang out and hit an evergreen tree that was partially protecting Cochise.

Realizing the shooter was now trying to shoot Cochise, I quickly undid his reins that were tied to Thunder's saddle and spun him in the direction down the trail back toward the Timber Lake Trailhead and Trail Ridge Road. I took my buck knife and quickly cut the straps holding the panniers as I could see the confusion and fear in Nickey's horse's eyes. Once I had freed the gelding of the heavy load, I smacked him on his ass - hard - and fired my Ruger Mini-14 once into the air to get Cochise moving and hopefully out of harm's way. Cochise needed no more prodding as she took to the trail as if her tail had been set afire.

From the safety of an evergreen tree shielding me from the shooter's direction, I watched Cochise as she rounded a bend in the trail and finally disappeared from sight. Thinking for now Cochise was safe, I turned my attention back to my assailant and Thunder.

Looking east, I saw no movement or flash of light to give away the location of whoever shot at us. The woods were still and silent except for the labored breathing of Thunder. Thunder was still alive and while I was getting Cochise cut free of the panniers and to safety, she had lain down on her side and was facing me. Her wide-opened eyes were looking at me as if she wanted me to do something - something to help her. From my position behind the evergreen tree, I could see the blood was flowing from her chest wound at an ungodly rate with pink bubbles of air foaming around the wound's entrance. It was obvious from the bubbles that one of her lungs had been punctured.

I knew Thunder was in horrible pain and going to bleed out, and there was nothing at all that I could do to save her. Feeling hopeless, I felt I had to do something. The very thought of putting her down broke my heart, but I knew it needed to be done. I could not however do it from a distance. I needed Thunder to know that taking what remained of her life was not in malice, but in love.

Moving stealthily around from the evergreen with my rifle at the ready, I made the short distance back to Thunder and once having done that, I lay down next to her and looked into her eyes as she looked into mine. Once I had got within her eyesight, I could feel a calmness come over her even though she was still struggling to breathe. Thunder, just like all horses, didn't care about how rich their owners were or how pretty or ugly they were. Thunder lived in the moment and as long as I treated her with kindness and a loving hand, she returned it tenfold with love and affection. With tears that welled in my eyes, I pulled my pistol and placed it gently between Thunder's eyes. Thunder knew what was happening, and I saw resolution and sadness flicker in her eyes, but I also saw understanding that she knew from the bottom of my heart I loved her so. Speaking in a calming voice, "I guess my friend I have never gotten over the 'I love Thunder phase.' It has been my pleasure to love you and for you to take me on as your friend. I have never known a better horse, nor will I ever meet such a gentle soul as yours ever again. Goodbye, until we meet again!" Having said what I needed to say, I pulled the trigger.

With Thunder's suffering now at an end, I wiped the tears from my eyes and cleared my mind of everything other than that which was needed to stay alive. My focus returned as did all my senses. I could feel the slight wind as it flowed over my body, bringing the aroma of the late autumn mountains. The air smelled of decaying autumn's leaves, snow, mud, and pine needles. The temperature was chilled, but above freezing. The sky cleared with the clouds moving south and forever blue stretching over the distant horizon and the Never Summer Mountains. All of this I considered as I thought about the shooter.

My enemy, whom I believed to be Samael Amos, may be moving into a different position to get a shot at me even though I thought this unlikely since he had targeted the horses intentionally when he could have just as easily targeted me. My gut was telling me that the game had just started and removing the horses from the playing field just evened the score. The shooter wanted me on foot, for that is how he played the game. To win the game was obvious, and that was to stay alive with your opponent dead. It was the ultimate game of life and death - one my adversary had played before.

I was still looking toward the east and scanning the tree line, wondering what my next move should be when a voice spoke out from the dark timber with an almost echo chamber tone, "Who are you?"

It was a man's voice and thinking he already knew where I was, replying in kind would not give away my position, but it would help me pinpoint his since I was not exactly sure where he was. So in a loud and confident voice, I spoke to the trees and the wind and the man hiding there. "The question is 'asshole' who the hell are you? And why did you shoot my damn horse?"

There was only mountain silence for almost a full minute before the shooter hissed his reply, "You know who I am and you came looking for me. No sane person would ride into these mountains this time of year unless they were on a mission of some sort. I know you are all alone because I have been watching you for several days. What has me baffled is whether you are the law, a bounty hunter, or a man bent on some sort of vengeance? So which are you - cowboy?"

Of course it was Amos and when he was speaking, I could pinpoint the direction and roughly where he was, but still could not see him. I did not believe he had moved since shooting Thunder and had stayed in the same spot observing what I would do. "Samael Amos, I came looking for you and my name is Dane Lee."

For several seconds the woods were quiet and then Samael spoke once again now with that tone of an echo chamber. "Dane Lee? Undersheriff Dane Lee of the Grand County Sheriff's department?"

Speaking once again in a calm and confident voice, "One and the same Amos - one and the same."

After hearing laughter for several minutes and hearing Amos alternating in between a malevolent hiss and the echo chamber tone, he replied once again, "I know all about you Dane Lee and your family and the ties you have to these mountains. Just last month I read that book that fellow wrote about your great granddaddy. Now your Granddaddy Matt Lee - the Ghost - lived a life I envy. He knew what life and death were all about and was not a man who you trifled with. A great man your granddaddy was, and I am honored you came looking for me. You know you can never arrest me Dane Lee; surely you have figured that out by now!"

Hearing this man talk about my family even if it was praise he used, brought my blood to a boil. Grandfather obviously, just as Amos had said, was a man you did not trifle with, but he was much more than that. This lunatic Amos in his all-or-nothing game of life and death in the wilderness, had not a clue about my ancestors or grandfather and what made my family down through the years the men they were. What he would never understand was we were part of the life and energy of these mountains. That our blood was the life force and spirit of all that is here and my ancestors were part of something bigger than ourselves. Just like the aspens, evergreens, elk, deer, and wolves, we were what made the Rocky Mountains something holy and sacred. When grandfather and the Lees spilled blood of their foes, there was always a righteous cause for doing so. Just like grandfather, I rode into these mountains to set a wrong - right. Amos killed Micah, Gene, Craig Dale and the others and almost killed Nickey Lynn as well and would not get a free pass from me. He had to pay for what he has done and the price was his life. Speaking to Amos hiding in the timber, I let that be known. "Amos, I am not wearing my badge and I am not here to bring you in for trial. Make no mistake Samael Amos, I am here to take your life!"

CHAPTER 32

An hour passed and nothing from Amos. He had quit talking and the dark timber that surrounded me was silent as the time of noon passed into afternoon. In the last hour dark clouds that had the look of snow had moved in from over the Never Summer Mountains, and the temperature dropped to just below freezing. Still crouched down next to Thunder, I could feel her body start to lose its warmth which drove home the fact that Thunder had also died at the hands of Samael Amos. Amos had a lot to account for even before he killed my horse. Thunder's death just became the last reason why justice must be done the mountain man way.

My stomach growled and reminded me I had eaten nothing since breakfast. Standing slowly, I now scanned in every direction, looking for movement or the telltale sign of any kind that would give away Amos' position. He had enough time since he last spoke to have moved into any direction. Since this morning I had gone from being the hunter to now being the hunted. It was not a pleasant thought, and my mind was working overtime trying to reverse that trend. In short order, the advantage had been tipped into Amos' favor. The worst part of it was I was also on his playing field - his killing grounds.

Palming my 357 Ruger as it slid easily and quickly into my hand, I checked the loads again and made sure the chamber was loaded under the hammer. I had no reservations about shooting Amos if it came down to that, and I had confidence in my ability to use the six shooter if needed. My thought was that if Amos wanted to shoot me from a distance, he could have already because he had more than an ample opportunity. He wanted to take my life up close and personal just as he had with all the others so it would be more satisfying to his sick mind. As that thought wandered through my brain pan, my stomach grumbled again, and if I was going to check out of this life today, I did not want to go on an empty stomach.

The good news was when I had lightened Cochise's load by cutting the straps on the panniers, I still had all my provisions and several full canteens of water. So I might as well cook me some grub while I was waiting for Amos to make the next move. After I had gathered the stones, kindling, and wood for a cooking fire, in no time at all I had a fire and began to fry up some bacon and beans. If Amos was going to watch me from a distance, he would have to watch me eat. Amos must have thought by not speaking again and disappearing into the woods that I might become fearful. I had learned to conquer fear a long time ago and one of those things I learned was you can't sit around stewing about it and you just had to face it and keep yourself busy. So screw Amos and his game playing. I was going to eat some much-deserved lunch. After pulling up a down log to the campfire, I rested my Ruger Mini-14 within grasp and made sure my right gun hand remained reasonably free as I went about the important business of feeding my grumbling stomach.

When I first rode here into Rocky Mountain National Park, I thought I had the advantage of surprise; what I did not consider was timing. Amos was right, for no man in his right mind would have ridden here this time of the year without some mission of sorts. He knew these woods better than any man alive since he worked here every day. I never had any advantage and I would be fooling myself if I thought I did. The way I saw it now the only advantage I now had was Amos wanted to kill me up close and personal and unlike Micah, Craig Dale, and the others, I knew the rules of this game were life and death. They did not.

As noon turned into late afternoon and then into early evening, a snowflake touched my cheek and melted and as I looked heavenward, it appeared as if the Rocky Mountains and I could be in line for a big snowstorm. Tossing a couple of more logs onto the fire, I could feel the temperature drop even more and I knew from past experiences here in the Rockies it would be a cold, snowy, and dark night. My gut instinct was telling me that was when Amos would make himself known again.

The snowfall was steady with nickel-sized snowflakes, and the next hour passed slowly as I watched the snow accumulate on the body of Thunder to about three inches. I kept adding logs to the fire and as the daylight slowly faded in the western horizon, I tried not to look directly into the fire for the fear of it causing me momentary blindness. As I waited, I ate a half pound of beef jerky and a can of peaches as the snow increasingly fell from the sky. If not for Thunder's death and Amos hanging back in the mountain shadows waiting for the right moment to strike, I could have been at peace here in the Timber Lake area.

The snow got heavier as the darkness came over the campsite, so heavy in fact the tree line surrounding my campsite was becoming blurred in the low light. As my circle of sight and light became less and less as the snow fell, the advantage tipped increasingly towards Amos. There was no doubt in my mind that during this night he would make his presence known. I was as ready as I would ever be. Every five minutes or so I would stand and stretch and walk around the campfire to keep my muscles loose. When the moment came, the worst case would be that I would get a cramp of some sort in my legs or arms. So I kept loose and ready and kept my eyes peeled to the surrounding woods, for I did not know from what direction Amos would make his attack.

The night and the hours grew long, and doubts now passed through my mind that maybe Amos had left the area knowing full well I was armed and seemingly knew how to use my sidearm. Then again, this whole scenario was possibly Amos' whole plan of attack. As the darkness stretched toward morning, I was becoming more tired and I now feared that my alertness was starting to wane. Each passing moment of wakefulness was making it more difficult to stay awake. I thought my strategy in waiting for Amos to make the first move was now flawed. And it was becoming clearer I may have bitten off more than I could chew.

The soothing snowfall and the warm fire were not my friends tonight. Catching myself nodding off for several seconds or maybe even longer, I realized that doing so would be the death of me, so I rapidly gained my feet and walked around the campfire again. Halfway around the fire I heard several tree limbs snap as something or someone was moving in my direction from the south toward the camp. If it was Amos, he was doing a piss-poor job of sneaking up on me. Palming my six shooter, I waited in anticipation as another tree limb snapped. Whatever it was making its way here was large, possibly larger than a man and I now doubted it was Samael Amos.

Now with my full attention focused on the woods and dark timber to the south, I heard the undeniable snort of Nickey's horse Cochise as she zigged and zagged back through the evergreens. Once Cochise breached the circle of light given off from the campfire, she saw me and in a moment of joy, she pawed the snow with her right hoof and she snorted more than a dozen times in happiness of finding me.

Even though I scurried Cochise away in an attempt to make sure she did not meet the same fate as Thunder, I was plumb happy to see her. There was no doubt in my mind that Samael Amos had seen Cochise as she entered my camp, and I feared that he once again would try to shoot her. Walking up to Cochise, I could see in her eyes the determination that no matter what I did now, she would not bolt again. She was here to stay by my side come hell or high water. I was just going to have to accept that fact and go with the flow of whatever fate had in store for Cochise and myself.

Walking up to Cochise, I gently grabbed her reins with my left hand when she went to bucking and snorting and on one downside of his buck, I could see the reflection in his eye of someone behind me. Palming my Colt, I spun 180 degrees to meet my adversary.

CHAPTER 33

As lightning quick as my draw was, the slick snow hampered my spin, causing one foot to give out and losing my balance which was all the advantage Samael Amos needed in his all-or-nothing attack on me. Amos was able to close the distance while I was trying to gain my feet and easily kicked my Ruger 357 out of my hand, sending it spinning until it landed in the snow.

With my handgun now useless and buried in six inches of snow, Amos slammed into my chest with a ruthless force with his black handled Buck knife in his right hand with the whetted blade pointed at my chest. I was able to block his downward knife thrust with a death grip onto his wrist as we struggled and wrestled matching each other's strength. Amos was heavily muscled and strong; there was no doubt about that, but I was an equal in that department.

As we fought chest to chest with neither gaining an advantage, I could smell his breath which smelled of wood smoke and burnt meat. His eyes were glazed over with a maddening look of a demented killer, and I knew this fight would only have one winner.

Cochise was spooked but did not bolt as she scurried here and there out of the way as Amos and I fought for control of his Buck knife. I had relied heavily on my 357 and that was turning out to be a huge mistake in this battle to the death. My knife was still in its scabbard hanging from my belt and useless to me now. I needed to create a space and a slice of time between the crazed killer and myself so I could also pull my knife.

Amos and I were both still on our feet as we wrestled with our arms locked in battle, and I could see in his eyes he was astounded he had not taken me off my feet yet. This attack on me had not gone as those had before. He must have been used to the quick strike and sudden death of his prey, but this time his prey had known the rules of the game and was somewhat ready for his attack.

What seemed like forever, but I knew only to be a couple of minutes, I felt that Amos was weakening little by little and that gave me what I needed to dig deeper for more strength and endurance as inch by inch I moved him backwards and closer to the campfire's flames dancing in the slight wind and consuming the energy of the wood with a maddening fury.

After I more than once moved Amos backwards, he also dug deep within himself and found the strength to stall our advancement toward the fire, but each time through muscle and sheer will power, I overcame him and once again I was able to keep him moving closer to the fire.

We were so close to the campfire now I could feel the heat on my bare hands, and I knew it had to be worse for Amos since his body was shielding me from most of the blistering heat. Suddenly Amos let loose and I shoved him hard as he tried to roll backwards through the fire with some success. He came quickly to his feet on the other side with only a small scattering of hot ashes and burning embers being sent skyward into the falling snow. The separation gave me time to pull my knife. I had never been in a knife fight before but had trained with my father and had confidence in my ability.

Now that I was armed just as Amos was armed, this battle to the death became more of a cautious one as we moved away from the fire still facing each other with our knives in an underhand grip with the killing ends pointed at each other as we circled looking for an edge - that momentary fail of the other that would give one of us the advantage to attack.

As we circled each other looking for that slight opening that would give one of us the upper hand, Amos several times lunged forward looking for my weakness only to realize there was none and he would suddenly pull back when he realized that I was ready for him. Samael Amos' face was like stone and there was no invitational smirk that one might expect in such a duel nor was there any fear on the man's face. His mind had drifted back to a primitive state, but his eyes showed his killer instinct. He had done this before and he liked it; there was no doubt about that. I had to match that killer instinct if I was to survive and have my revenge on the one that had brought so much death and misery to the ones I loved. I had to win this battle to avenge Gene, Micah, Craig and the others. Most of all there had to be a reckoning for what Amos had done to the woman I loved - Nickey Lynn.

Samael Amos in this fight was no longer human; he was an animal that was moving and thinking only on instinct. And once again in his intense animal state, he rushed in with a sudden burst of speed, and this time he did not pull back. In an upward thrust I could feel the edge of his knife as it cut through my Tempco down coat and the flannel shirt beneath and drawing blood - my blood. It took several seconds for the pain to register, but the son of a bitch had cut me. Not a puncture wound, but a slice down low in my side and just above my right hip. Up thrusting my Buck knife with my right hand missed, and I only stabbed the air, but it was close enough that Amos pushed off and we both tumbled backwards several feet.

During my stumble backwards, I backed into Cochise, who was in a panic as the fight progressed and now with the smell of blood in the air, Cochise went to bucking and I fell underneath him. I did not have time to worry about Cochise stomping me with his hooves because Amos saw his advantage when I went down hard and with his knife raised in a killing blow, he fell on top of me.

Amos' savage downward thrust was meant for the center of my chest where my heart was, but I was able to roll my shoulder to thwart that killing stab; thus, instead of my chest he caught the top of my shoulder just below my neckline and once again sliced through my coat, shirt and muscle.

Once again, it was a cutting and not a puncture wound, but this one was deeper than the one on my side, and I could feel my warm blood as it flowed from the wound. With Amos still on top I grabbed his right wrist and stopped a second deadly thrust of his Buck knife.

In my struggle to keep Amos from stabbing me again, I realized I had lost my knife once I had fallen under Cochise and now it was just my strength against Amos' strength, but he was the only one with a knife. My wounds were bleeding badly and my strength was becoming weakened by the blood loss as I could see Amos' glistening knife point inch closer with my death forthcoming.

Cochise was still on top of us as she snorted and reared up more than once, which was what saved my life. During Cochise's panic, he reared up and intentionally or not, kicked Amos just below his chin. The first kick stunned Amos, but the second one as Cochise came down from the height of his buck caught Amos once again, this time on the back of his head, and I saw the lights go out in his eyes as Amos succumbed from being kicked in the head twice. He fell to his side like a discarded scarecrow.

Not knowing how badly Samael was hurt, I tried to regain my feet quickly, but fell twice as my right arm gave out as my muscles failed from my wounds when trying to push off to stand. I lay back down trying to gather my wits and willpower to try to stand again. Lying face down, I could now feel the chill and the wetness seeping through my down coat and shirt from the mud and snow that Amos and I had fought in.

Cochise, now that the fight had come to a sudden stop, moved off to one side about ten feet and was snorting heavily as he tried to come to terms with what had just happened as was I.

Knowing Amos might not be out of the fight completely, I knew I had to move and with sheer willpower, I pushed off with most of my weight on my left arm so that I could gain my knees and then my feet.

Having gained my feet, I finally saw where my 357 had landed as the barrel was sticking out of the snow. As quickly as I could which was not quick at all, I moved over to it and almost blacked out when I bent over to retrieve my 357 pistol. Checking my loads and feeling satisfied I had a working weapon, I pointed it at Amos and moved closer to him as he still lay where he had fallen.

As I got closer, I could see the telltale sign of his breathing as his coat moved slightly up and down with each breath. He was alive even after getting kicked in the head twice by Cochise. Pointing my pistol in a one-handed grip at the still alive Samael Amos, I now had a decision to make.

CHAPTER 34

I stood for several seconds over the still form of Samael Amos and more times than I could count, the thought of just shooting him passed through my mind and each time I decided to pull the trigger, I never put enough tension on the trigger to shoot and kill the man. I wondered if I had lost my killer instinct or if I ever had it to begin with. If any man deserved to die, it was Samael Amos, but for now I couldn't do it.

My right side and the top of my right shoulder were throbbing, and I could feel the warm, sticky blood as it dripped off which told me I needed to get the bleeding stopped or I would be in no condition to make any type of decision regarding Amos. First things first though I had to secure Amos.

After I moved over to the panniers I had cut off of Cochise, I kept the killing end of my pistol pointed at Amos while rummaging through them and finding what I was looking for - two sets of my Grand County Sheriff's handcuffs. I walked cautiously over to him, and he had yet to move; he was still in the sprawled position he had fallen in, and from his breathing pattern, I knew he was still out from the knockout kicks by Cochise. Holstering my weapon and as quickly as I could in my wounded condition, I handcuffed both of Amos' wrists behind his back and after taking his boots and socks off, the other set of handcuffs went on his ankles.

Feeling that Amos could no longer be a threat, I went about trying to stop my bleeding from my wounds inflicted on me by Amos during our fight. After scraping enough tree moss from the trees surrounding the campsite, I began to plug the wound in my side. Each time I poked the moss in, a severe throbbing pain would shoot up my side and made me grimace with every agonizing poke of my finger. After about ten stuffing's of tree moss, I could no longer feel the blood flowing from the wound and felt it was just as good as it would get. While I worked on my wounded side, the blood from my shoulder was dripping off my elbow since I had my arm bent in such a way that the elbow made the lower part. The snow surrounding my feet had turned crimson with my lifeblood as it leaked out staining and melting the snow.

Turning my attention to my shoulder wound, I felt dizzy from the blood loss, but packed tree moss into that wound as well. The large artery that flowed in the region had not been severed or I would have already bled out by this time. I knew that was good news but that did not, however, lessen the fact that there was still a possibility of bleeding out if I did not get the shoulder wound stopped. Each and every time I packed more moss into the wound, it caused me to almost black out as the pain would overcome my awareness. My breathing was shallow and Cochise looked on with wide eyes as if she was wondering if I would live or die. After about the fifth time of packing another layer of tree moss into the gaping wound, I could feel the darkness overcoming my mind. My legs became heavy and then I lost my footing and fell back into the snow and mud.

The wetness of the now falling snow felt good on my face. I blinked several times to clear my mind and to help find my way through the brain fog I now found myself in. The sun had moved considerably since I had blacked out and it was now midafternoon. It would seem that I had been out for at least four hours, possibly more. Suddenly I remembered what had happened, and I rolled to my side to see what condition Amos was in.

Amos was wide awake and was staring at me with his cold eyes and once he saw me looking directly at him, he spoke in a calm, but an eerie voice, "You know Dane Lee, if not for that damn horse of yours, I would be eating your liver right now to enrich my soul with your power. I had you beat and your soul was mine."

Amos was still handcuffed, and he had woken up with not too much ill effect of getting kicked in his noggin twice by Cochise. He had scooted himself over into a sitting position with his shoulder leaning against an evergreen tree. This was the first time I had ever heard him speak up close, and his voice brought chills to my inner soul. I could feel the malevolence that surrounded him and his whole essence stank of evil. My gut was telling me that Samael Amos was not human, but something else.

Gingerly, I could work myself into a sitting position as I studied Samael. His clothes, as were mine, were wet and muddy from the fight. His hair was also caked with mud and mixed with what looked like a considerable amount of blood from where Cochise had kicked him. His pupils were black as midnight and dilated. The whites of his eyes were bloodshot to the point of looking pained. He was injured and handcuffed, but his demeanor was still threatening. There was no doubt in my mind that Amos, though handcuffed, could still be a deadly adversary.

Without replying to Amos, I slowly stood and looked skyward toward the heavens and said a silent prayer that somehow I was still alive. The Ute Great Spirit and the Lord Ole' Mighty must have seen the trouble I was in and brought Cochise to my rescue which saved my life.

The snowfall that had awoken me was getting a tad heavier and by the look of the sky, the snow had settled in and was not moving on anytime soon. My campfire had consumed all the wood that had been left for it, but the ashes and embers still smoldered. Grabbing more wood, I pitched it on the fire. And it was not long before the fire took hold of the new wood and I had the makings of a good warming campfire.

Still keeping an eye on Amos, I moved toward Cochise and grabbed his reins and brought him closer to the fire. Taking my wooden curry comb, I began to work his tail and mane not to groom him, but to reassure him that all was well. Cochise's eyes never left Amos as he could feel the presence of evil as I could. Having felt that Cochise was as calm as he was going to be given the circumstances, I fed him some grain and some sugar from my stores in the panniers.

Having taken care of Cochise, I stood about fifteen feet away from Amos as I tried to work out in my mind what my next move was when Amos spoke again in his unnerving echo chamber voice. "You know Dane, you are not that much different than I am. You think you are, but I assure you that you are not. Man by nature is evil, for in reality he is just a beast no better than those that roam these woods in search of prey. They teach us from a young age how to be good and to keep the evil that lurks in us all at bay; some learn the lesson - some don't. Some let the malevolent seduce us; others like myself romance it until we are one and the same. You have it as well deep within your soul Dane Lee, just like your Grandfather Matt Lee had it."

I blinked my eyes twice, for this animal to mention my grandfather had surprised me, and in a confused voice I asked, "My grandfather? What he did those many years ago was what he had to do. You know nothing at all about my grandfather and the righteous battles he fought."

Amos laughed and then he spit some blood in my direction which fell short before he yelled at the top of his voice, "I read that damn book about him! He walked on the dark side as do I! He knew what it took to be the best in the bringing of death! He killed all those Ute Indians way back when...because he...LIKED IT! He cut their ears off to mark his prey and if the truth be known, I would bet he ate their livers for their warrior power! Like I said Dane Lee, you are more like I am than you would care to admit!"

There was no question that Samael Amos was insane, but what he did next unnerved me some. After his rant about my grandfather and the evil that is within us all, Amos began to scream at the top of his lungs an unholy sound that pierced my very humanity. This new voice of rage sounded as a wounded and caged wild animal. Once he stopped his immoral scream, he looked at me with all his hatred within his being and began to flay himself violently back and forth onto the ground as if the devil somehow possessed him. He fought and yanked on the handcuffs to the point that I thought he might even find the strength to break them and let him loose once again into the world.

Just as suddenly as he had started violently flopping back and forth onto the ground, he stopped. His wrists and ankles had taken a severe beating from the metal handcuffs and were bleeding profusely now. By instinct only I had quickly palmed my Ruger and had it steadily pointed at the head of what I knew now was the devil himself. Speaking again in his unnatural and surreal voice, he hissed, "I don't live in the darkness Dane Lee - the darkness lives within me!"

CHAPTER 35

Amos looked at me with those black pupils, and I felt him as he probed my spirit inside me which unnerved me even a little more. He stared at me for a full minute while I held my Ruger steadily at his head before he spoke again with an immoral smirk on his face. "You think you can kill me, Dane Lee? Sure, you can kill this body, but know forever my crux lives on. You must have guessed I am immortal - right? My core, my essence has lived down through the ages of time and time again. I have seen and brought more death, misery, and destruction than you can ever imagine, Dane Lee. I fought shoulder to shoulder with Leonidas and the other 300 Spartans as we brought death to thousands of the Persians at Thermopylae. In the 1600's it was me that brought about the Ulster massacres in Ireland. In the 1700's in Pennsylvania it was me at the Penn's Creek massacre. I have seen it all Dane Lee and now for the shocker Dane Lee - I was there on Marble Mountain in the Sangre de Cristo Mountains where the legend of your Grandfather Matt Lee began. La Caverna Del Oro was where it began for your grandfather, but it was a small stop in time for me Dane Lee. In the 1900's I thrived in that prison hell-hole called Andersonville in Georgia. These moments and many more moments in history I have seen. All of it - all the deaths and destruction - was glorious my friend. Join me Dane Lee and feel the power of life and death; be immortal and walk the dark path as I have. Evil is one hell of a teacher, Dane Lee. All you have to do is listen, feel, and understand its supremacy. Release me and I will show you how you can live again and again!"

I stood mute for several minutes as I appeased my nerves. Watching and listening to this man brag about things he said he has done down through the ages and his boastfulness brought a clearer mindset. There was no way in hell that this man, beast, or devil would walk out of these mountains alive. It was now just about how and when. Holstering my Ruger 357, I felt more empowered than I had when Amos had started talking since Amos' rant about evil and immortality had gotten me over the moral hump that was cluttering my conscience. Speaking calmly, clearly, and loudly enough so that there would be no misunderstanding, "I remember in sixth grade reading a quote by Albert Einstein that I have pondered many times since becoming a law officer. 'The world is a dangerous place to live; not because of the people who are evil, but because of the people who do nothing about it.' You are not the boogeyman Amos; you are a man just like me. You breathe the air and you bleed red just like me. Granted, you are one malicious son of a bitch with delusional visions of grandeur about who you are to mask the fact you are just a common low-life killer. Well, my friend, your reign of terror ends right here in the cold and snow in Rocky Mountain National Park."

Amos' eyes never left me, and his smirk was still cemented on his face as I spoke to him and after I was done for the time being, he laughed that bone chilling laugh trying once again to spit on me which fell several feet short.

As I glanced toward the western horizon, the snow was steady but the wind had died to a whisper. The sun above the snow and clouds had finished its daily arc and was trying to settle down for the night behind the trees and the mountains. Looking back at the man that had killed my horse and friends and had almost killed my love Nickey Lynn, I spoke once again. "Been a long day Amos with all this fighting and you trying to spit on me. Since you are not going anywhere soon, I believe I will rustle up some grub."

My wounds were throbbing as I went about the normal chores of a campsite, but looking back at Amos, I knew there was nothing at all normal about this campsite. Amos' look of insane hatred continued, but he said nothing as I threw a couple of more logs on the fire and got me the fixings for supper.

Checking my wounds, I found that they had stopped bleeding and the cold mountain air would help in my fight against any infection. After fighting hand to hand with a deadly adversary, I considered myself lucky to still be alive.

After frying up some bacon and beans, I sat down on a log I had pulled up next to the fire and began to eat. Mopping up the grease from the bacon with some store-bought tortillas, I looked over my shoulder at the dead body of Thunder, and there now were about eight inches of snow covering her body. Looking back toward the killer of Micah and Gene, I stared at him straight in the eye and continued to eat. Amos was still handcuffed and was more than twenty feet away, leaning on an evergreen tree trunk which was too far away to get any benefit from the warming campfire.

As I studied Samael Amos, he looked cold and his bootless handcuffed feet were turning blue. I had to hand it to him; he remained quiet about his obviously uncomfortable position with his hands handcuffed behind him as well. His wrist and ankles still bled from when he had struggled against the cuffs, and the snow beneath was crimson with his blood. It bothered me not one iota. My humanity in regard to Samael Amos was no longer present. My given feelings at this moment were as about as neutral as one could get. There was no anger, nor was there any happiness as I watched the man with the black eyes suffer from the now cold and getting colder night.

Amos suddenly went into another fit of devil possessed flopping back and forth on the ground as his black pupils rolled up in his eyes in a vain attempt to free himself for a full five minutes. Just like the last time he did this, I palmed my Ruger just in case he found the strength to somehow break the chrome chain of the Grand County Sheriff's handcuffs. There now was no doubt in my mind whatsoever that if he broke loose, I would shoot him deader than hell. There will be no courtroom, judges, or plea bargains. Justice of the righteous was here and now, and it was going to be served at the end of a 357 Ruger or the Rocky Mountains themselves. Sometimes justice is served cold and brutal; this was the justice of my ancestors.

Amos' insane flopping quit and this time it looked as if he had broken his right wrist as the blood was flowing even at a faster rate than before. After holstering my weapon, I saw that he once again took up staring at me with that evil smirk on his face again. His feet were already blue and now had a blackish tint to them as the snow and cold continued on into the night. Amos' breathing was becoming shallow and was a sure sign of hypothermia setting in. I felt no remorse, and he would get no sympathy from me. I could almost feel the ghost of grandfather standing over my shoulder urging me to slit Samael Amos' throat in the old way of the mountain. I fought that urge to end it quickly, for something inside told me that there was more justice in letting the mountains and the cold extinguish his life.

Wanting a few answers before this evil monster was gone from this time and place, I asked him a question. "Samael, according to your trophies of drivers' licenses pinned to the wall of your cabin, Micah Trask was the first. Was he?"

Amos' eyes searched my face in the flicker of light of the dancing flames before he answered in a rather calm voice considering the circumstances. "Micah? Micah Trask? What was Micah to you Dane Lee?"

I took a full minute before answering as I studied Amos' face. He was genuinely curious why I was asking about my best friend. "Micah was my best friend since childhood. You took his life to feed your madness, and he was one of the reasons I rode to Timber Lake looking for you!"

A smile slowly crossed Amos' face and then he laughed his eerie and bone chilling laugh before he replied, "One of the reasons Dane Lee? You are a law officer, but you are not wearing a badge. I knew you were here trailing me not because it was your job. It had to be personal. Let me guess Dane Lee. The girl at the cabin was your woman as well! I could smell your stink on her. It pleases me I took her life as well! What you do now will never bring her back! You want revenge my friend, but her death will haunt you forever since you were too slow to get there to save her!"

CHAPTER 36

Samael would not have known Nickey had survived his brutal attack, for he had fled into the mountains following his attack on Nickey and Gene. He would have assumed he had killed her since the wounds he had inflicted on her normally would have killed most anybody.

Not wanting to tell Amos that he had failed in killing Nickey just yet, I wanted to focus on Micah. Speaking in an even tone, "Why Micah? What made you pick him?"

Amos' eyes locked on mine again as the snow had fallen off some and in a voice that sounded as if he spoke in an echo chamber, "Something marked him just as those that followed. They could not see it; no one could see the mark, but me. The mark became visible, and it beckoned me to take his and the others' lives to feed my own. I realized your friend and the others were marked by something greater than myself. I knew they were men of valor and had strengths that normal men did not have. They were marked to feed my soul and to give me what I needed to stay immortal. Micah was the first of those that was marked. In the course of doing my job, I had seen him as he strutted through the park as if he owned it. Having asked about him from the rangers that were locals, I heard he had been a mighty warrior in the jungles of Vietnam, so he became my first feeding. Since Micah had been marked, I needed to take his life and eat his liver for his warrior and mountain man power. Simple Dane Lee, Micah and the others needed to die so I could live!"

How Amos in his madness had hidden it from the outside world for so long baffled me. He had held a job and gave wilderness tours to the public, and the whole time he was insane. He had given me some answers and some insight into his thoughts and the more I heard, the less I understood. His belief he was immortal was something out of a bad horror movie. There was one thing that had me confused since reading Craig Dale's book, so I asked Amos about it. "Those lives you took - Craig Dale, Bryan Amen, Jerry Toney, Randy Weems, Shawn Lord, Kevin Kyriss, and Micah – had all gone missing and I presumed killed on a Saturday here in the park. Why Saturday?"

Amos' black eyes widened as he looked at me and his voice was no longer an echo chamber, but a hiss. "You are a fool Dane Lee. A bigger fool than I thought. You have been confused by something so unassuming. Now Dane Lee, you are not worthy of taking this life. Saturday, you ask? Saturday was my normal day off you dupe."

If the circumstances had been different, I might have chuckled at Amos' response, but here in the remote wilderness and with the snow still falling, there would be no laughter.

I looked at the man I had handcuffed, and his blood from when he fought the handcuffs had stopped flowing. His bare feet now were blackish and even though I was not a doctor, I would say they were already near frozen. The hypothermia of uncontrolled shivers had started as Amos' inner core temperature plummeted. The temperature, since the sun dropped out of sight, had fallen to well below freezing and was still getting colder.

Hypothermia had killed more than its fair share of folks that ventured into the high country during the autumn and winter months. Weather at this altitude was so unpredictable it caught most people off guard. I believed Samael Amos was no longer in any condition to flip-flop on the ground anymore in a crazed, possessed state. Amos' eyelids were getting heavy, and his breathing was still shallow as the mountain cold was taking the life out of Amos. I felt no remorse in letting the Rocky Mountains claim this killer of my friends. It did not please me; I only felt it was justifiable in this case. Samael Amos' reckoning was close at hand and death awaited him.

Tossing two more logs on the fire brought Amos out of his deepening slumber, and he spoke once again in his echo chamber voice. His words though had become slurred as death was creeping toward him. Amos' eyes found mine again in the darkness lit only by the dancing flames of the campfire. "How did you come to suspect me, Dane Lee? What was the slip-up that led your deputies to come to my cabin?"

I almost laughed at Amos' questions and before answering him, I got off my log near the warm fire and strolled over to him. I bent down so he could see my face. Voiced with authority, I told him the truth. "That's the funny part in all of this, Samael; we did not suspect you. The last man you killed Craig Dale had been writing a book called 'The Daunting' about folks that had gone missing in Rocky Mountain National Park. He listed your name in some papers along with those men you had killed. We thought Craig Dale had contacted the local supervisor of the park – you Samael – for research for his book and nothing else. When Craig Dale had been reported missing, we were just following up on his note he left with your name. We didn't suspect you until you killed Deputy Sanford and almost killed Nickey. I would call you a 'dupe' Samael, but I do not think you would appreciate the irony of that."

For several minutes Amos looked at me with those black, cold, and deadly eyes, showing nothing as he pondered what I had said. Then his eyes blinked and showed understanding, and a smile crept across his face as he looked deep into my eyes. Once he had thought through what I had said in his slowed by hypothermia mind, he once again laughed in that uncanny echo chamber tone that sent chills and goosebumps down my arms and made the hair stand up on the back of my neck. Now speaking in that hiss he sometimes used, "I thought the law had sent those two weaklings to arrest me for doing what I was meant to do. I realized my reign of 'the bringer of death' during this life had come to an abrupt end. I fended off and killed those that meant to extinguish the malevolence that lives within me. How more wrong could I have been?"

Palming my Ruger 357, I pressed the barrel hard into the center of Amos' head and spoke with no anger and in a neutral tone. "Don't flatter yourself, Samael. You panicked just like any normal lowlife killer that realized his game was up. That is all! You are not some wicked, supernatural, immortal evil that roams the ages. You are just a man that is delusional and thinks he is something more than he is."

Still with my Ruger pressed into Amos' flesh of his forehead, I looked down at the crimson snow where Amos had injured himself fighting the handcuffs. I then added, "You bleed red just like me Samael, and your death is forthcoming and your flesh will feed the animals as they scatter your bones across the Rocky Mountains. You will become dung and scat for the bear and the wolves. What's left will turn to dust in time, and the death you had wrought will forever be forgotten. And all those whose paths you have crossed will soon forget all the memories of you. You are not the boogeyman or the devil; you are a man, nothing more."

Amos' eyes searched mine not in hate, but in an acceptance of his pending death. His voice was no longer a hiss. It had reverted to the echo chamber mode. "Pull the trigger Dane Lee and feel the ultimate power of God and the Devil of taking a life. The everlasting war of good versus evil is right here and right now. Pull that trigger and end this life so I may move on to the next. You must know Dane Lee it will not end here; we will meet again. Pull that damn trigger you fool!"

Believe me, the thought of blowing Amos' brains out crossed my mind more than once as I had the barrel against his forehead. But instead I holstered the Ruger and in a voice with no remorse, "I will not give you the satisfaction of a quick death, Samael. The mountains deserve to give you a slow death and so it will be!"

Amos' eyelids once again became heavy and the uncontrollable shivers of hypothermia began. Based on my experiences in these mountains, I knew it would not be long before his life would be snuffed out by the cold.

Looking toward the darkened sky and the falling snow, I felt at ease with my decision of letting the mountains and the snow claim Amos' life. It seemed sort of fitting he would die here in the Timber Lake area which had been his killing grounds for Micah and the others.

As I waited for the slow death to take its victim, I said my goodbyes once again to Thunder as the snow was now about ten inches covering her body. I remembered Thunder as bringing me joy because she brought me in close contact with her grace, beauty, fire, and spirit. My emotions were running the gauntlet of confusion. I was not sure how to act anymore and if I should curse the heavens or embrace them. Cochise was standing close enough to the fire to gather in its warmth, and he seemed just as confused as I was on the events that were unfolding as the night progressed.

Amos' shivers had succumbed to an almost peaceful slumber as the cold death was closing the gap. Walking back to him, I thought he had already died, and I bent down to feel his neck for a pulse. Once I touched his cold neck, his eyes opened. And in a slurred and dying voice Amos asked, "Dane Lee you said 'almost killed Nickey;' does that mean she did not die?"

Bending closer to his ear so he could hear me, "You failed in killing my only true love. Nickey lived and will make a full recovery. Just know as you become food for the bears and wolves, she will live a rich life regardless of what you did!"

Another bout of the shivers racked the dying body of Amos. When the shivers stopped, he spoke his last dying words in an almost silent whisper. "Understand Dane Lee that in my next life I will come for you…and her!"

CHAPTER 37

I woke up to the sound of a mountain chickadee as it sang its song of happiness through our open bedroom window.

Rolling over, I took in my morning pleasure of watching the woman I loved as she slept. Her breathing was slow and regular. Even in her sleep Nickey had a hand over her cheek hiding her scar where Samael Amos had cut her face. She was bothered by it and others could see it, for it was in plain sight. Most times when I looked at her, I never even realized it was there until she tried to hide it. The scar mattered not, because Nickey Lynn Lee was still the most beautiful woman in the world in my eyes. At our wedding last December, she wanted to wear a bridal veil to hide it but agreed to my wishes and did not. It was a beautiful and spiritual Christmas wedding that took place on Christmas Eve.

I decided to let Mi Vida sleep a tad more since today was May 2nd, 1977 and a huge day in her life as she returned to work with no restrictions as a Grand County Deputy Sheriff. She would be nervous, but I knew the woman she was and she would be just fine. Her nightmares about being attacked by Samael Amos, after Gene had been killed, came less and she was sleeping more peacefully. Over time, her body had healed and her mind was just about there.

Rolling to my back, I realized my dreams of what happened about the death of Samael Amos at Timber Lake were less frequent. My mind was healing as well, and life in front of Nickey and I looked promising.

I rode Cochise out of Rocky Mountain National Park and told no one - not even Nickey - what happened in the cold and snow in the area surrounding Timber Lake. Nickey knew in her heart what transpired, but each time she would bring it up, I would change the subject. In the last two months she had not brought it up at all. My cover story for the death of Thunder was that an illegal poacher had accidentally shot my mare in the park and I could not locate the shooter during an all-encompassing snowstorm. My story to Sheriff Walker was that my trip to find and locate Amos had proven to be a folly and had ended up in the death of one of my horses.

As far as it concerned the law, Samael Amos was still a wanted fugitive in the death of Officer Gene Sanford and the assault on Nickey. He also was wanted for questioning in the disappearances of Craig Dale, Bryan Amen, Shawn Lord, Jerry Toney, Kevin Kyriss, Randy Weems, and my best friend Micah Trask. I was the only one that knew the arrest warrant for Amos could never be served.

I closed my eyes and remembered my dream from last night as grandfather made another appearance. It would seem grandfather was still a permanent fixture in my dreams. Even though I never met him while he was alive, I felt I knew him better than anyone else could. In this dream and the many I have had since my incident with Amos, grandfather had no more urgent messages about death and enemies. He never spoke in any of my recent dreams, but he seemed happy that Nickey and I had tied the knot. To this date grandfather had not mentioned children to continue the lineage of the mountain men Lee's, but I knew it would not be long before he broached the subject. I think grandfather already knew Nickey and I were working feverishly almost every night in that regard.

Getting out of bed slowly so as not to disturb Nickey's sleep, I headed to the stereo for some morning music. Grabbing our new Conway Twitty album "Play Guitar Play," I played the hit single "I Can't Believe She Gives It All to Me" for what seemed the hundredth time since buying the album. The song reminded me of how blessed I was to have Nickey as my wife. *"I pinch myself when I wake up..."*

The morning went quickly as Nickey and I drank orange Tang with our bacon and eggs as we listened to the radio. The big news of the day was that the Denver Broncos' head coach John Ralston was fired after missing the playoffs with a 9 – 5 record. That reminded me that our own Middle Park Panthers did not fare as well after going 3 and 6 for the season. Football was in our blood and we looked forward to the Panthers' and Broncos' upcoming seasons.

Nickey's county sheriff Blazer was waiting for her at the office so she had to ride in with me this morning. After another glorious Rocky Mountain sunrise, the day started with not one cloud in the sky and with the sun already up in the eastern sky giving off its rays of warmth. There was a slight breeze which brought the pleasing scent of mountain pine into the Blazer as we drove down the highway.

Life was good with Nickey by my side as we stopped to feed and grain Cochise before work. When Nickey was using a curry comb on him to brush out his mane and tail, I walked over to Thunder's stall. Each time we stopped here, I always looked in to it as if with the will of God or the Ute Indian Great Spirit, I would find her there still alive and healthy. Just like the many times before, it was silent and empty. My heart hurt knowing I had to leave Thunder's body there at Timber Lake in Rocky Mountain National Park last October. The guilt weighed heavily on my heart about that. At the time I could not have risked going back and letting someone else discover Amos' body before nature did what it does best to make the body of Samael disappear.

When I reached the office, there was a warm and wonderful homecoming for Nickey. Everyone on duty had a small present for Nickey as soon as she had walked through the door. There were a few tears from Yvonne the dispatcher and more than a few from Nickey as she basked in the love of her coworkers. I caught Nickey several times glancing at the desk of Officer Sanford as if his empty work station drove home he was no longer coming back to work. Each time Nickey looked at Gene's empty desk, I could see the sadness reflect there of what had happened.

Sheriff Tom Walker was all smiles and gave Nickey a long extended hug and a small kiss on her cheek. Standing to the side, I could even see the hint of a tear in our boss's eyes while welcoming back Nickey.

Standing aside and not saying much of anything since this was my lady love's moment and not mine, I felt more in love with Nickey now than at any other time in our relationship. I was proud of her that after the brutal attack she had the courage to once again walk through the doors of the station to become a Sheriff Deputy again.

Walking out into the hallway, I left all the happy well-wishers and walked up to the bulletin board. Micah's photo with description was still there and like always I reached up and touched it even though I finally knew the fate of my best friend. Below Micah's missing person photo, there was a new photo and warrant for Samael Amos. His photo was a blown-up shot of him standing next to the Timber Lake sign in Rocky Mountain National Park. Amos' photo was yellow from age and very grainy, so the details of Amos' face did not stand out. The photo could have been taken of any man in a million. No way did the evil of this man show through in this photo; his black eyes looked distant and unrecognizable.

Just as I was studying Amos' photo, Sheriff Walker had left the small gathering of party goers and strolled over next to me. In a voice of authority of my boss he said, "Dane, I need to talk to you in my office."

Once in Tom's office, he motioned for me to close the door and then pointed toward the seat across from his desk for me to take a seat. I did both knowing that from his tone and demeanor that what was forthcoming was not about Nickey's homecoming or the weather.

Sheriff Walker opened a manila folder, and he shuffled through some reports inside for several minutes before speaking. Closing the folder, he leaned forward and put his forearms on his desk. His reading glasses were tipped down on his nose to a point they were almost ready to fall off. Looking over the top of his glasses, the sheriff still in his voice of authority, "Dane, two weeks ago several hikers found the scattered bones of a horse and a saddle in the remote Timber Lake area. The saddle had your name stamped into the leather underneath the back jockey. So it would seem the remains of your mare Thunder have been located where she had been shot when you rode into the park last October."

The sheriff paused for a full minute studying me as if gauging my response or waiting for me to say something. I knew this day had been coming and in reality it surprised me it had taken so long to happen. My face stayed neutral, and I said nothing.

Sheriff continued as before, "You had reported that someone had shot your horse when you had ventured into the park so this was not a surprise to anyone. However, there was something else in the report that is a huge surprise. The same hikers found other scattered bones and the big surprise a human skull. We both know countless people go missing each year within the Rocky Mountain National Park and most times they do not find the remains and almost always when they are found, we have no way of determining who the skull belongs to. The person who had met their death in the Park is still reported missing."

Once again the sheriff paused, and his eyes were searching mine looking for insight and answers. I knew from his demeanor he now suspected the truth of what happened back in October. He might not know the details, but he knew. The sheriff finally asked me a question. "I was wondering what you make of all of this?"

Still staying neutral and vague, I answered his question. "Well Tom, I find this all very interesting, but I assume there is more in that file you read."

Tom was still looking over the top of his glasses and remained silent for another minute before replying. "Your assumption is correct, Dane. They found a wallet about fifty yards from the human skull and 100 yards from Thunder and your saddle. In this wallet along with some credit cards was a driver's license. Samael Amos' driver's license to be exact. I cannot help but wonder Dane how your saddle and horse came to be in such close proximity of what looks to be the remains of Grand County number one fugitive Samael Amos."

Still looking for my response, the sheriff took a breather to gauge how I took this news. Since Tom had not asked a question, I remained silent until he continued on. Sheriff Walker, after two full minutes, reached into the file on his desk and produced a single sheet of paper. He read it silently and once done, he placed the paper back in the folder and spoke again. "The human remains that were found had been sent to the Grand County coroner's office. Our coroner Ken Stockton as you know is top-notch and knows his stuff. His report has a very interesting observation - not fact - just an observation. It would seem some human remains recovered were bones that make up the wrist and the ankles of the departed. It would seem that these bones had considerable trauma on them. The report showed that there were many deep cuts across the bones. His observation was that...this is his quote, 'It is possible that the departed had been wearing handcuffs at the time of death.' Now that is not a fact and Mr. Stockton will not testify in court it was, but it is an interesting tidbit. The reason I got you in here Dane is that I am wondering if you have anything to add to this file. On the record or off the record, you decide. Is there anything you want to say?"

Rolling it around in my thinker, I knew there was no hard evidence I had left Amos to die from hypothermia or it was he who shot Thunder. Even if Sheriff Walker decided to pursue the matter with more investigation, there would never be a case against me. I still had no regrets in letting Amos succumb to the cold at Timber Lake. Justice in my eyes was done and over with. Amos had died knowing full well I knew he had killed Micah, Gene, and the others. His attack on Nickey had been avenged. My soul was at rest with what happened. I cleared my throat and in a clear and a not remorseful voice I answered Tom's question with, "I reckon not."

My answer just affirmed what Tom already knew that there was more to the story than what was in the file sitting on his desk. Much more, and I was the only one who knew the truth. Pushing the file to the side, Tom leaned back into his chair and with an almost silent sigh he spoke again, "I guess Undersheriff Lee that this is another case for which we will never know all the answers. And I am okay with that. You are dismissed."

Standing up, I opened the door and before I could step through it Tom spoke once more, "Dane, glad to have you and Nickey back as a team here in the sheriff's department."

Turning I said nothing, but nodded "yes" knowing this was Tom's way of letting me know this matter with Samael Amos was now a closed case.

Walking out of Tom's office, I was in a not very agreeable mood having to lie by omission by not telling the sheriff the truth about what happened to Samael Amos. I knew it was better left unsaid and for the mountains to only know the truth. My mood improved when I saw Nickey sitting at her desk and right then and there I knew it justified everything that had happened at Timber Lake. My victory over evil was now complete having Nickey healthy and as my wife until death do us part. She was my life, and I would live it with her no matter what. As I got closer, I could hear a song that was playing softly on the radio at her desk and once again it proved my life had a soundtrack. The song "If" by the band Bread was an oldie, but still one of my favorites, *"If a picture paints a thousand words..."*

As I sat down in the extra chair near Nickey Lynn's desk, our eyes locked on to each other as we both sang almost silently along with the radio *"The words will never show..."*

Yvonne the dispatcher broke our loving moment and our song when she yelled into the squad room, "Dane you got a phone call from some man who is saying he needs to talk to you right now. He sounds sort of creepy. He is not taking 'no' for an answer and keeps calling back."

Nickey said in her singsong voice, "You are the popular one this morning, Dane. First the Sheriff wanted to talk to you in private and now some 'creep' wants to talk to you. Next thing you know you will be signing autographs for all of your groupies."

Nickey and I both laughed with my mood now doing a 180 degree as my love for this woman overrode all the unpleasant thoughts of Samael Amos. Looking back toward the dispatcher, I said, "Yvonne, please transfer the call to Nickey's desk. I will take it here."

Less than thirty seconds had passed when the desk phone rang and I answered it on the first ring. "This is Undersheriff Dane Lee. How can I assist you today?"

There was static on the line as if the call was made from a great distance and it was several seconds before the voice on the other end hissed, *"Dane Lee?"*

The call was confusing from the crackle and pop of static, and I could not decipher if the bad connection caused the "hiss" or not. Answering the question I said, "Yes this is Dane Lee."

The line cleared and the static was no longer bothersome; a voice, from out of my not so distant past that I thought I would never hear again, sent goosebumps down my arms and in a malevolent echo chamber tone said, *"Soon Dane Lee, I will come for you...and her!"*

Kurt James

Dane Lee's grandfather Matt Lee was first introduced in the James western adventure Rocky Mountain Ghost. Here is a sampling from Chapter 5 of that book which is available on Amazon.

Rocky Mountain Ghost

It almost felt good to talk about it after all these years. Clearing my throat, I began again, "That morning that Tom Driscoll had faded into the wilderness, the five of us began to talk at length and with more seriousness about going to find the La Caverna Del Oro. It was an adventure for the young and as it turned out for the not so very bright.

That morning during breakfast we all began to recall the clues that Driscoll had laid out in his tale about the location of the cave of gold. We knew it was roughly 150 miles west of us in the Spanish Peaks region and supposedly on the newly named Marble Mountain. After making a pact, the five of us decided to give it one summer to look for the lost cave and to see if the legend was true.

After deciding that was what we were going to do, we wasted no time in informing our employers William Bent and Ceran St. Vrain we would be leaving. And with a halfhearted laugh, we told them we would be back for trapping season penniless and broke looking for work. They assured us we would be welcomed back with open arms.

Being used to having to pack our mounts in a hurry, we were able to head west and into the unknown about midday. We were jovial and in high-spirits. It was good to be on such an adventure with those that could easily be your brothers.

All I recall about the trip to Marble Mountain was that it went well and after about eight days or so we found ourselves camping at the base of Marble Mountain. The country and the lay of the land was new to us, but it was still the Rocky Mountains and all five of us lived and breathed the Rockies.

From our vantage point as we rode from the east, we could tell that the top of Marble Mountain was well above where the trees never grew anymore. Possibly 3,000 feet or more above timberline. According to the tale, as it was told by old man Driscoll, the cave of gold was located just above timberline and on the southwest side of the face of the mountain. With no other clue to go by and all of us knowing this was probably a folly and a one in a million chance, we were nonetheless game and ready for the adventure. We headed to the southwest side of Marble Mountain.

It was on the third or fourth day of exploring the southwest side that I started to see the crows. Never more than one at a time and I was never sure if it was the same crow or not, but it or they seemed to be watching us. I brought it up to the others at supper and they laughed at me and kidded me for being scared of my own shadow. Of course I laughed it off also with my friends, but when Sam began to play his harmonica that evening, I could not shake the feeling that we were being watched from close and afar. I had difficulty sleeping that night because the sounds of the woods and timber were different, I could not put my finger on it, but the sounds of the wilderness had changed. I kept my new Hawkins rifle close and the powder under the buffalo robe I used for sleeping to keep it dry. My gut instinct was telling me something was off kilter in the woods that surrounded us.

The next morning after some dried venison jerky for breakfast, we set out again to explore and Mike Sands saw it first and yelled for all of us to come running. What he discovered was an ancient fortress at the mouth of a small cave. And I mean ancient like 300 years before ancient. The walls of the fort were constructed of rock and timbers, and rifle pits had been constructed for its defense, which led all five of us to suspect that Driscoll's story of the Spanish legend and the three monks was in fact a true telling of an antique but not forgotten story.

Dan Buxman found an old tarnished brass Spanish helmet and breastplate and handed the breast plate to me with a huge grin. I could not help but notice it had a hole in it roughly where the heart of the person that had been wearing it would have been.

Since the ancient fort we found was just below timberline and according to the tale told by the old man Driscoll, the La Caverna Del Oro was above timberline, we set out to explore above the old fort. Once again a crow or "the" crow landed in an evergreen directly in front of me and watched me as I rode by him. Now looking back after all these years, I now know it was a warning and I did not have the wherewithal to understand it then. With an odd feeling of dread, I continued on and upwards with my friends.

Within a couple of hours, Jay Edwards had found the entrance to a much larger cave. As we all bunched up to check out the cave, we were excited and more than positive it was La Caverna Del Oro - the Spanish lost cave of gold. There was a faded but apparent red Maltese cross marking the entrance to the cave. We were all dumbfounded, knowing there was a small chance of ever finding the cave, but here we were and destiny had led us straight to it.

We were obviously jovial, laughing, and punching each other in the arms about our find, but since it was well past midday and we were all hungry, we decided to make camp at the entrance and fry up some venison steaks and beans from our supplies. The others spoke of what they would do with our new found riches even though we actually had not found any gold yet. I was quiet and reserved with the feeling of dread overpowering me. I kept my eyes on the tree lines surrounding our camp. We had tied our horses and pack horses to a picket line in between two trees and I kept an eye on them also.

After a filling supper of venison steak, Sam Walters broke out his harmonica and started to play a merry tune. I tried to join in the festivities of the moment, but I failed as I remembered something the old man Tom Driscoll had said and we all had seemed to forget. Others believe that the Indians now protect the mountain and the demon cave after being directed by their "Great Spirit" to stop anyone from ever stepping foot in the cave again.

Remembering this part of the tale, I felt that overwhelming sense of foreboding again and decided to bring it up to the others as soon as Sam's merry rendition on his harmonica was over.

It turned out sooner than ole' Sam and the rest of us ever imagined as an arrow pierced his throat dead center of his arms as they were raised holding and playing his harmonica. The remaining four of us were slow in moving as we were all in some sort of shock momentarily as we watched Sam gurgle on his own blood and paw at the killing arrow in his throat.

The next to go down was Dan Buxman, as more Indians than I could count stormed our small encampment; Dan took a lance through the back that pierced him through and through.

Maybe because I had been on edge already because my gut instinct had told me things were off kilter, I had my Hawkins rifle loaded and primed, and I shot and killed the Indian that had killed poor Dan.

Out of the corner of my eye, I saw Jay Edwards taken off his feet as two of the wild Injuns tackled him; he really never had a chance as they went to work on him with their killing tomahawks.

Mike Sands and I were also attacked by numerous hostiles, and we were giving them all they wanted with our tomahawks and skinning knives. In the initial onslaught, I had cut and cleaved two, and Mike had taken down three as we fought for our lives in front of the La Caverna Del Oro.

We had a few moments to catch our breaths and after the first rush of hostiles, we looked at each other knowing this was our day to die and we nodded at each other as only friends can do in the face of certain death. Death awaited us and as true warriors, we knew that we were not going to make it easy for those that wanted us dead. Taking my weapons and swinging my arms back and forth in front of me to limber up, I was ready and even willing as the next wave of hostiles rushed in at us.

Covered in blood and not really knowing if it was ours or theirs and with our Hawkins now useless and forgotten in the battle, we fought like savages and madmen slashing and hammering with our skinning knives and tomahawks. I lost count of how many Indians we either killed or maimed in those moments of blood lust and at the height of the battle in front of the demon cave. All the while during the blood, killing, and slaughter we were being pushed back closer and closer to the entrance to the cave.

I saw Mike go down to one knee as one of the hostiles was able to hit him at the top of his shoulder with a tomahawk. Seeing my friend and brother Mike still fighting from this now almost defenseless position, I fought and killed my way to his side and was able to grab him and lift him back to his feet. Out of the corner of my eye, I saw the darkness of the cave and I grabbed Mike and rushed headlong into the darkness and the entrance of the La Caverna Del Oro."

THE DAUNTING

Kurt James poetry can found on the website Creative Exiles –

I was a man born out of time and a century or two too late; I should have been a Mountain Man. Growing up in the foothills of the Rocky Mountains in a time before video games, cell phones and iPads was a learning experience that kids nowadays will never know. We played outside until the sun went down, and our mothers would shout out from the front steps for us to come home. My summer nights were filled with "hide and seek" and "kick the can." Summer days were filled with riding our bikes and exploring the outer regions of our neighborhood and beyond with our best friends. Shooting BB guns, fishing, tubing, catching crawdads and guppies were our everyday events. More often than not, we would pitch tents and camp out and watch the stars hoping to catch a shooting star. My friends and I would tell tales of ancient times of bravery and honor of those that walked our mountains before us. Our heroes were mountain men. Men like Hugh Glass, Jim Bridger, William Sublette, Jim Beckworth, and Jedediah Smith.

As a youngster there were two things that changed how I would forever look at the world. The first was reading Jack London's "Call of the Wild." The second was a movie starring Robert Redford "Jeremiah Johnson." Jack London and Robert Redford cemented my love for all things wild and good ole' Mother Nature. The poem below is my salute to the mountain men that dared go where no man had gone before.

Mountain Man

Rocky Mountains spoke to him, saying his name,
Packed his Hawkins rifle, headed there to lay his claim.

Indians fought, pelts to trap, weather to tame,
Many years passed a Mountain Man he became.

Freezing rain, harsh winter, waist deep snow,
Cold temperature and frost bite took many a toe.

Scars on his scalp from a female panther swipe,
All alone, no give up in the man, he wasn't the type.
More years passed, winters seemed longer,
Wishing for the time, younger and stronger.

Never once thinking about heading down below,
No way in hell, leave his loved mountain plateau.

His 40th winter, he died, gave it his all, everything he was
worth,
Living the life he chose, Rocky Mountain marrow of the earth.

By

Kurt James

AUTHOR'S NOTE

If you, the reader, has made it this far, that means you have finished reading my book "The Daunting," and I would just like to take a line or two to thank you for purchasing my work, and I hope you enjoyed this Rocky Mountain mystery and tale of retribution of Dane Lee and Nickey Lynn.

It is my hope you have found Grand County, Colorado to be full of living and breathing characters such as Dane, Nickey, Gene, Samael, and of course Matt Lee also known as the "Ghost." I love Colorado and especially Rocky Mountain National Park.

I also wanted to assure you that the Colorado geography, along the path my heroes Dane Lee and Nickey Lynn Chavez traveled through Grand County, Colorado, as well as the Rocky Mountain National Park do in fact exist - every mountain, mountain range, mountain pass, river, creek, and all the towns mentioned in this tale.

I took some liberty in using the modern names in some cases or the more historical names if I thought it fit the story better. I wanted folks who were locals or familiar with these Colorado areas mentioned in the book to be able to follow along on Dane's as Nickey's trail of clues more easily in their mind and to be able to travel if they wanted to on horseback, foot, or even by car or 4 wheel drive the same path of Dane Lee as all trails headed toward the remote mountains of "The Park."

ABOUT THE AUTHOR

Kurt James "The Colorado Storyteller" was born and raised in the foothills of the Colorado Rocky Mountains. With family roots in western Kansas and having lived in South Dakota for 20 years, Kurt James naturally has become an old western and nature enthusiast. Over the years Kurt James has become one of Colorado's prominent nature photographers through his brand name of Midnight Wind Photography. Along with being a member of Western Writers of America, his poetry has been featured in the Denver Post, PM Magazine and on 9NEWS in Denver, Colorado. Kurt James' poetry is also featured at Creative Exiles, a collection of some of the finest poets on the web. Kurt James Reifschneider is also a feature writer for Hubpages with the articles focused on Colorado history, ghost towns, outlaws, and poetry. Inspired at a young age by writers such as Jack London, Louis L'amour and Max Brand, Kurt has formed his natural ability as a story teller. "The Daunting" is Kurt James' fifth novel, but not the last novel of the wild and dangerous Colorado Rocky Mountains. Kurt James is currently working on his next Rocky Mountain adventure called "Conner's Saga" which will be the fourth installment of Kurt James' Rocky Mountain Series.

Follow Kurt James on Facebook, Twitter, and his author page on Amazon.

Made in the USA
Middletown, DE
19 July 2019